the 20th Christmas

the 20th Christmas

Andrea Rodgers

A Novel

AMBASSADOR INTERNATIONAL
GREENVILLE, SOUTH CAROLINA & BELFAST, NORTHERN IRELAND

www.ambassador-international.com

The 20th Christmas
© 2014 by Andrea Rodgers

ISBN: 978-1-62020-269-2
eISBN: 978-1-62020-370-5

Cover design and typesetting: Hannah Nichols
E-book conversion: Anna Riebe

AMBASSADOR INTERNATIONAL
Emerald House
427 Wade Hampton Blvd.
Greenville, SC 29609, USA
www.ambassador-international.com

AMBASSADOR BOOKS
The Mount
2 Woodstock Link
Belfast, BT6 8DD, Northern Ireland, UK
www.ambassadormedia.co.uk

The colophon is a trademark of Ambassador

DEDICATION

For Joe, Logan, and Krissa

ACKNOWLEDGEMENTS

Thank you to those who first recognized my passion for creative writing and helped me to learn and strengthen this area: my language arts teachers in elementary, junior high, high school, and college—especially Marilyn Rodgers, Mary Knock, and Lin Buswell. Also, my writing mentors in my twenties: Jodi O'Donnell and my Omaha critique group—Cheryl St. John, *lizzie starr, Barb Hunt, and Donna Knoell.

To all of my family members and friends who believed in me, especially my parents: Kathleen and Richard Hora, Joseph and Sebyl Motsinger. When I was a child, my favorite activity was sitting next to you on the couch as you read to me. Thank you for planting those first seeds.

To my husband, Joe, whom I married when I was twenty-three years old: You have been my biggest support with writing and all other areas of life. Thank you for bouncing ideas around with me while I worked on this book, providing feedback when I read it to you, and being Super Dad! You've always been there for me. I love you.

To my son, Logan, with whom I became pregnant when I was twenty-seven: you made me realize that there was something I enjoyed more than writing. I have treasured my days as a stay-at-home mom with you—you are my heart and kindred soul. Your personality inspired the character of Chase.

To my daughter, Krissa, with whom I became pregnant at age thirty: I am envious of your energy, determination, confidence, and humor! You bring such joy to my life with your sweet, smart, and polite spirit—you inspired the character of CeCe.

To those who helped me to write this book accurately: my dear friends Sarah Young, Melissa Hammerly, and Brooke Williams—as well as her friend Stana Donnelly—my neighborhood friend Erin Dahl and high school friend Dustin Gehring. I am very grateful for your time.

To Mindy Abendroth and her Mary Kay ladies for providing the motivation that I needed to write this book: Thanks to you, I heard God say, "Write this—it's time," after I woke up from having a dream.

I was ecstatic when Ambassador International offered me a contract and am so appreciative to Sam, Tim, and Alison Lowry for making my life-long dream come true! Thanks also go to Brenda Covert, my excellent editor, Hannah Nichols for the best cover ever, and Jennifer Ross, author of *Isaiah's Story*.

And last, but certainly not least, to all of the missing children and families who have lost their loved ones to abduction: You are in my prayers.

PART ONE

CHAPTER ONE

Wednesday, December 21, 1994

Chase? Where are you? Chase!

Panic filled Arianna Tate's chest as she searched the small café for her toddler son. The two had spent the morning Christmas shopping at a mall in Des Moines, Iowa, until fatigue took over Arianna's body and told her she must stop for a spiced latte on her way home.

She'd been holding her little boy's gloved hand when they stood in line to order and had smiled at him as they sang along to "Silent Night" on the radio behind the counter. The store was decorated with strings of multi-colored lights and silver and gold tinsel. A Christmas tree with red and green glass balls stood next to a window while light snowflakes fell outside.

Arianna let go of Chase when it was time to pay.

"Are you going out of town for the holiday?" the woman behind the cash register asked.

"Yes, we usually go to my parents' place—a couple of hours away."

"Well, stay safe—we're expecting a bad snowstorm on Christmas night."

After they chatted for another minute about the brutal winter weather in the Midwest, Arianna took the paper cup with one hand and reached out her other to meet Chase's.

Instead, there was only air.

Arianna whipped around, hat falling from her head, and her gaze darted quickly to every corner of the café.

"Chase?" she called out as she paced the floor. The weight of a black wool coat made her move too slow.

An elderly man sat at a booth and looked up from reading the newspaper, but otherwise the place was empty.

Hadn't there been a woman standing behind her in line? Where was she now? Had she seen where Chase had gone?

"Is everything okay?" the store clerk asked.

"I—I don't know where my boy is. He was right here."

Arianna ran to the employees' entrance and frantically looked around the back of the store. The clerk followed.

"Don't worry, ma'am, I'm sure he's here somewhere; little kids love to hide."

Arianna nodded, but tears blurred her sight. It wasn't like Chase to run off. He was an easy child. From the moment Chase had been born, her son was peaceful and sweet. Unlike every other mother she knew, Arianna hadn't minded getting up in the night to nurse her baby back to sleep. Eight hours was too long to go without seeing her precious offspring. She was giddy for several months after he was born. Arianna kept this news to herself because she felt guilty for being on a high rather than have postpartum depression when the mothers around her struggled.

Originally, she had been scared to have a baby. Arianna and Alan had married young, just days after graduating from college. They had met at a modern, non-denominational church on campus. While many of their peers were partying on the weekends and hopping from one bed to the next, Arianna and

Alan made it through those years without rebelling against the values their parents had taught them. They were each other's first date and first kiss, and their first time making love was on their wedding night.

They had planned to enjoy married life for a few years by themselves and to begin their careers before having children, but God had other ideas.

"I can't be a mother yet!" Arianna exclaimed after reading the positive pregnancy test just a month after their honeymoon.

Alan gulped, looking pale and thin behind his glasses. "It's all right. We'll manage. Somehow."

Life was surreal as the months went by. They went to doctor appointments together and heard the baby's heartbeat, saw Arianna's belly grow, and learned that morning sickness (the most intense nausea one could imagine) lasted *all day*. Full of self-pity, Arianna asked herself why was she in bed when she could have been rising to the top of the corporate ladder, having graduated summa cum laude with a degree in finance and marketing and certain to land a good job. But, just when she was starting to feel sorry for herself, she felt her baby kick. That was all it took. She knew right away . . . *that's my son.* It was the most special feeling she'd ever had. Nothing and no one could ever take that moment away. God had blessed her with the best gift she could imagine: motherhood.

Her instinct was right—she carried a boy in her womb. Chase Xavier Tate was born in February of 1993. He was a healthy 8 pounds, 12 ounces. His hair was blond, and he had a mess of curls before he'd even turned a year old. His eyes were blue—just like his dad's—and he had the same milky white complexion. Even his personality was a clone of Alan's—quiet, calm, and observant. There wasn't the normal grabbing or trouble sharing that Arianna thought all toddlers went through. She smiled every time she saw

Chase wait patiently for a toy that another child was playing with, and when he saw that a peer wanted something of his, he handed it right over, seeming satisfied that he had made a friend happy.

Arianna already worried about her son being a people-pleaser. His spirit was so sensitive, if she so much as raised her voice a little, the sparkle in his eyes dimmed and his cheeks pulsed as tears of shame followed. She knew all children were subject to change, but she was fairly certain that discipline wasn't going to be of much concern. He already identified when she was sad and offered affection to make her feel better—like the time she slipped on the kitchen floor and fell on her arm. Chase had been only eighteen months old, but he had dropped his building blocks to run over and embrace his mother.

Money was tight for the Tates on Alan's teaching salary, but Arianna didn't mind. She enjoyed every day of being a stay-at-home mom. Nobody seemed to believe her when she said that she never had a bad day—but it was true. She'd never felt angry with Chase, and they'd been blessed without illnesses other than colds and a couple of fevers when he was teething. There were many days when Arianna was too exhausted to feed him non-processed foods and keep the apartment clean, but she wouldn't trade their bond for anything. She could almost always tell what he was thinking and feeling, just as he seemed to be in tune with her.

That's how she knew that he hadn't run off.

She felt her airway tighten. She bent over but still couldn't breathe. A bell rang in her ears. It was a memory from a few minutes before: the jingling of a decoration on the front door. It happened whenever someone came in or out. The person behind her had left while she was paying for the coffee.

Who walks into a coffee shop and leaves without ordering?

Arianna ran outside and scanned every direction, feeling dizzy. Chase was not on the sidewalk outside of the store or in the parking lot.

"Ca-call the police," she whispered to the cashier who had followed her. "My son. My son has been kidnapped."

CHAPTER TWO

What was he wearing?

Does he have any birthmarks or unique features?

Do you have a recent picture with you?

The questions that she'd been answering for the past several minutes buzzed like flies around Arianna's head. She stared at the two police officers with her mouth frozen and her limbs shaking.

This is Iowa! It's a safe state! How could this have happened?

Arianna was relieved to see her husband arrive in his black Ford Tempo.

"Alan!" she sobbed as she hugged the man whom she'd been married to for two and a half years and had known for four.

"We're going to find him," he said matter-of-factly. However, this was one time when she knew her usually-calm husband was just as wrecked on the inside as she was.

"Then let's go! *Let's go!*" Arianna pushed past the officers, ready to run through the streets again, as she already had before they'd arrived—but the cops reached out and stopped her.

"We have already notified our detectives. The best thing you can do right now is to give us every possible detail of information. Can you describe the woman who was standing behind you in line?"

Arianna shook her head at the taller cop, Officer Jon Buchannan, while tears flooded her cheeks. She had never looked back. She'd been preoccupied with choosing which latte to order, counting her money, and making sure the cup hadn't slipped through her fingers when taking it from the person behind the counter.

"You didn't hear Chase make a sound? He just went with her? Do you think it was someone he knew?"

Arianna wanted to wake up from this horrible nightmare. How could she be such a bad mother to chat about something insignificant with a stranger rather than notice her son being taken? The whole situation didn't make sense—it was as if he'd just vanished.

"I-I don't know. I mean, I can't imagine who . . . we don't know that many people in this area. We just moved to Des Moines in July for my husband's new job. She must have had something to entice him. I would have noticed if he was just *grabbed* from next to me! Oh my . . . oh my . . . I need to get out of here!"

The shorter cop, Officer Christopher Sparks, was the one to stop her this time. "Mrs. Tate, there is nothing you can do right now. The good news is that usually women kidnap because they can't have a child of their own. There is a good chance that your boy is not being harmed. Our detectives are getting his picture out. He'll be on the news tonight, and you can make a plea that hopefully will get the kidnapper to come to her senses and return Chase."

Friday, December 23, 1994

As soon as Arianna's parents heard the news about Chase, Phillip and Gloria Sanderson drove over from their small town in eastern Iowa and stayed at a hotel when they weren't at the Tates' apartment cooking, cleaning, and offering hugs. They assisted Alan and Arianna by holding a candlelight vigil. It was cold—twenty-six degrees—but bearable for local residents to show their support with helping to find Chase.

Alan spoke into a microphone. "We are so appreciative for all of you who are here. We know that this is a busy time of year and that most of you had plans with your family, so it really means a lot to us that you came."

They were outside the coffee shop where Chase had last been seen. The owner had offered to do anything she could to help find the little boy. Inside the store, she was providing free coffee and cookies, and volunteers were passing out flyers.

Officer Buchannan came, off duty, with his wife and two teenage children.

"We're going to find him," he said confidently to Arianna.

On the day Chase disappeared, the detectives from the Des Moines Police Department had called in the Division of Criminal Investigation, so Arianna hadn't expected to see or talk to the initial officers again. She was touched that Jon Buchannan was at the vigil.

"Thank you," she said quietly, looking down at her black boots.

The special agent on the case had assured her and Alan that someone would most likely come forward once Christmas was over—after hearing or seeing suspicious behavior from a family member or acquaintance. Many people tended to be so focused on shopping for gifts and getting ready to host holiday gatherings that they didn't pay as close attention to the news this time of year. However, the increase of families getting together gave them an advantage for someone to notice a child that didn't make sense in their circle.

Law enforcement had thoroughly searched the café, just in case Chase had accidentally gotten trapped somewhere—and brought in search hounds that lost his scent outside. They'd even looked inside dumpsters, which made Arianna's stomach turn.

She'd heard of children playing in refrigerators or unlocked cars and not surviving . . . but which was worse: to have him pass quickly into the arms of the Lord or to have him survive but hurt somewhere?

Instrumental Christmas music played from somewhere in the distance, and Arianna looked away from all the bright candle flames and up to the sky. She hadn't slept well the past couple of nights and had a sensation that she was flying. If only she could. She'd certainly fly far away from here.

"How are you?" her mother asked, coming over and using her hand to brush Arianna's hair away from her face.

Arianna blinked and looked at her mom. "You know that saying, God doesn't give us more than we can handle? I don't believe it."

The older woman nodded. "I know, honey. No mother should ever have to go through this."

"I don't want to live if it's without him." Arianna wiped her eyes with her sleeve. "Tell me how this is ever going to be okay? How is it ever going to make sense if Chase never comes home . . . or we find out that horrible things have been done to him?"

Her mother's nose turned red. "I know that there's nothing I can say to make you feel better. But there's that Bible verse from Romans: For I consider that the sufferings of this present time are not worthy to be compared with the glory that is to be revealed to us."

Arianna stared for a moment at her mom, feeling numb, and turned away toward a group of women approaching her.

"We're so sorry. We're all mothers, and this has hit us really hard," one of the ladies said. "I can't believe someone would take a two-year-old from right next to you. Is *any* place safe anymore?"

"Do you think there is a connection to the Johnny Gosch kidnapping?" someone else shouted.

Arianna remembered the story of Johnny Gosch from 1982 because they'd been the same age at the time of his disappearance. He was a twelve-year-old newspaper carrier in Des Moines who never finished his route and was never seen again. The missing case had sparked a fear campaign in the Iowa schools. Students were taught almost daily about stranger danger—so much so that many children thought it wasn't a matter of *if* but *when* someone would try to lure them to a place where their bodies would never be seen again.

Finger-print kits were handed out and a "secret word" was to be demanded from anyone trying to pick up those whose parents were unable to come for them.

Chase hadn't been old enough to be taught about stranger danger.

Was there something deep inside of Arianna that had known she would someday experience a child abduction firsthand? Even before the Johnny Gosch case, she was on guard.

When Arianna was six, she had a best friend named Rose. The girls lived on the same street, three houses apart.

It was a typically humid summer day for Iowa when Arianna ran barefoot in her swimsuit to knock on Rose's door to see if she wanted to play in the sprinklers and plastic pool set up on the lawn. While waiting for someone to answer the door, she scratched a mosquito bite and studied the chipped pink polish on her toenails.

A red car drove by, and Arianna looked up to notice that the driver was a guy with dark hair. The car slowed down as soon as the man and Arianna made eye contact, and then the car turned into the next door neighbor's driveway. It made her nervous how the male continued staring through his window. Arianna stood unmoving on the front step, finally remembering that her friend was on vacation.

The red car reversed out of the driveway, turned back to the direction of Rose's house, and stopped at the curb. Arianna twirled her long hair between her fingers. The driver stepped out of the car and walked toward her.

But nobody's here. And I don't know him. Why is he coming this way?

Her breathing quickened. She didn't give it another thought— she ran through the yard as fast as she could to her house. She was sobbing when she slammed the door behind her, locked it, and ran upstairs to her room where she shut her blinds.

"What is it? What happened?" her mom asked as she rushed into the Raggedy Ann & Andy-themed bedroom.

"There—there was a man," Arianna whimpered, pointing in the direction of Rose's house.

Gloria's face darkened. "What do you mean?"

Arianna took a deep breath. "He stopped his car and walked up Rose's driveway—so I ran."

"Wait here."

Arianna watched her mother walk outside to the middle of their yard and raise her hand to make a shield from the sun as she squinted in the direction of Rose's house. A moment later, she was back inside.

"There's no one there now. Probably a door-to-door sales guy."

Arianna nodded and felt her body relax. That is, until the next week after Rose came home from vacation.

"I was riding my bike yesterday," Rose said after a sip of lemon-ade, "and a red car followed me home!"

A tickle on the back of Arianna's neck made her shiver. "Did you say a red car?"

"Yeah."

"Was there a man driving?"

"Yep. With black hair."

They could never prove it, but they had always believed they were possible targets that summer. Had it been a warning to be on the lookout for sinister people in the future? Arianna wasn't naïve; she should have known better.

It's all my fault that my son is gone!

Alan shook his head at the man in the distance. "No, there's absolutely no reason to think that there's a connection to Johnny Gosch," he answered. "And please don't live in fear because of what happened to Chase. That only means that evil has won. It has always been around us, and it always will, trying to prevent us from enjoying life and to stop focusing on the good. To make us have self-doubt and lose our faith. Let's prove that the good in the world is stronger as we all work together to bring Chase home."

Arianna looked vacantly at her husband before turning toward the crowd. Many eyes were staring at her, and faces blended together into a blurry mix. She walked around Alan.

"Excuse me. I'm going to go inside the store and get a cup of water."

She kept her head down as she walked, not wanting to see one more look of pity on another's face. Not wanting to hear one more person tell her how sorry they were. She didn't want to be here. Didn't want this to be real. She was supposed to be at home with Chase right now, helping him make his first gingerbread house.

Her mother had gone inside the café minutes before and was now sitting at a table with a cup of coffee.

"Do they still put children's pictures on milk cartons?" Gloria asked, her short blonde hair perfectly in position. Her bony hands were clutched on her lap and posture straight as always, but her usually-smooth face was splotchy and tired.

"Not really." Phillip Sanderson ran a hand through his dark hair and stood up from sitting next to his wife. He grabbed a toothpick from a box on the counter and chewed the end as he stared, transfixed on something outside the window.

Arianna remembered learning in school that the Missing Children Milk Carton Program had begun in 1984 but had fizzled out due to the uncertainty of whether it actually led to the return of those featured—and also to put an end to the fear campaign.

"Then how do people in California or New York know to keep their eyes open for Chase? He could be across the country by now."

"Mom, please. Stop," Arianna whispered.

She loved her parents dearly and was grateful to have had them around for this agonizing and terrifying time, but she was craving space. As much as she dreaded being alone after Alan returned to school after winter break—how was she going to survive days by herself that had been centered around her little boy for almost two years?—Arianna knew it was probably best that her mother and father head home before the expected snowstorm on Christmas night so that she could get her bearings. They insisted they would be back to keep her company as soon as they could. Chase was their only grandson, and they were taking the tragedy as hard as she and Alan.

The television, which had been on quietly in the café, took everyone's attention when the newscast music started.

Two days prior, Alan and Arianna had stood in front of cameras and held each other close as they pleaded for the safe return of their little boy. The sound bite was being repeated regularly on all local affiliates with a picture of Chase taken just weeks earlier when Arianna had ordered photos at a chain photography studio for his upcoming second birthday. The blond, curly-haired child held a Thomas the Train toy and grinned from ear-to-ear. If money wasn't an issue, they would have had professional pictures taken every few months, but this had been only his second photo shoot. She longed to have a nice camera to capture Chase at every phase, and now that he was gone, she realized that she didn't have nearly enough photographs of her son.

The next shot on the screen was of the elderly man who had been reading the newspaper at the booth that day. "I really wish I had seen something. I wear bifocals to read the paper, but my eyes are useless for far away. Can't stop thinkin' about that mom. It's so sad. Hope they find that little boy. Saw his picture—cute kid."

The news anchor spoke in a serious tone: "Witnesses recall seeing a woman in line behind Arianna Tate around the time of Chase's disappearance. Police would like this woman to please come forward. She is not considered a suspect, but they would like to question her on what she remembers from that day, no matter how little the details."

Phillip snorted. "She better be a suspect—or *person of interest*—if I have anything to say about it."

The owner of the coffee shop turned off the television. "The very fact that she hasn't come forward makes it seem even more certain that she's the kidnapper. Wouldn't an innocent person want to help immediately?"

"Unless she doesn't watch TV. Or was visiting from somewhere far away," Arianna mumbled, filling a cup with water from a cooler.

"He's out there. Don't give up." Gloria stood up and hugged her daughter.

Arianna knew that her face was blank. "I don't really have a choice."

CHAPTER THREE

Sunday, December 25, 1994

Despite the Tates' appearing on television, passing out flyers, and holding the vigil, Christmas morning arrived without the return of their twenty-two-month old.

Alan had appreciated his in-laws' support; he missed his mom and dad terribly. Since their death in a car accident when he was twenty-one, he had never felt as desperate for them as he did this week.

Alan hadn't truly understood a parent's love until he became a father to Chase. It was a feeling of pure selflessness. Every morning he awoke with a purpose and soft heart; Chase gave Alan a reason to do everything with passion and love. He'd been willing to give up his life for Chase before his boy had even taken his first breath.

Arianna's labor had been quick and smooth until her pushing phase. It'd been ideal for a first baby—his wife was fully dilated in under three hours from when her water broke. Alan was impressed with Arianna's insistence at having a natural labor without an epidural or any pain medication. But, things had turned frightening when Chase's shoulders became stuck in Arianna's pelvis. It was too dangerous to perform a c-section by that point, and it took four hours of Arianna pushing before Chase entered the world—limp, purple, and silent.

Dear God, no, Alan had prayed while still holding tight to his wife's hand. *Let this child have a chance at life! Take mine if you must, but not my son!*

With the help of an oxygen mask and then a continuous patting on his back by the nurses, Chase began wailing. Alan's body nearly crumpled to the floor as he thanked the Lord for the miracle.

Now he tasted bile on his tongue. How many miracles with Chase could one father have?

Alan found his wife sitting in front of their Christmas tree, cradling a gift she'd wrapped in Thomas the Train paper for Chase.

"He's never going to get this," she whispered.

"Don't say that. Of course he is."

"No, Alan, do you know the statistics? Do you know that most children who are abducted by a stranger are never found? Or if they are . . ." Arianna choked as the now-familiar, hourly sobs made her body tremble.

Alan knelt down and pushed his wife's long, dark brown hair away from her face and then wrapped his arms around her tall, slender frame. For the first time since his son was kidnapped, Alan cried. He didn't have the strength to fight it anymore. The thought of never seeing his boy again was too much to take. He hadn't had a chance to teach him to play catch or ride a bike or even to give Chase his beloved G-I Joe toys that his parents had given to him during his own childhood.

He took off his glasses and wiped his eyes with his shirtsleeve, glancing at his watch. "Let's go to church, Ari; if we leave now, we'll make it just in time for the service to start."

Arianna nodded and laid the present underneath the artificial blue spruce that the three of them had decorated just weeks before.

As he locked the front door, Alan recalled fondly how Arianna had pressed the play button on their CD player—the first they'd ever owned—an early Christmas present to each other this year so that Arianna could purchase her favorite Christmas albums. Then, she had scooped Chase into her arms and held his chubby cheeks against her face as she swayed to Amy Grant singing, "Breath of Heaven."

"Angel!" Chase gushed, pointing to the tree topper that Alan was getting out of the box that had been stored in their hall closet. He appeared to be left-handed, and that same hand had his only birthmark: a small, circular dot on the outside of his palm.

Right now the Tates lived in an apartment, but whenever their next child was born, Alan hoped they'd be in a house. He planned to start a master's program in January that would eventually earn him a higher income.

"Here, Buddy, you do the honor." Alan had handed his son the angel.

"Whee!" Chase giggled as Arianna lifted her son so that he could complete the tree. They had strung popcorn, white lights, and candy canes on the branches. It looked perfect.

Life *was* perfect, as far as Alan had been concerned. They were happy, they were thankful, and they were at peace.

How could he and his wife feel so differently just one month later? How could their life have become so depressing without any warning? They had followed all of the rules during their twenty-four years, had walked a good path . . . why had God let this happen?

We must not give up faith, Alan reminded himself as they took their seats in church. They had been praying non-stop since their son went missing, but this was the first time they'd attended a service.

He noticed a toddler boy nearby with curly blond hair like Chase's. Alan felt as if his heart were sliced down the middle. He needed comfort; he needed a sign that everything was going to be okay.

But there wasn't one. He'd never had trouble concentrating in church before, until today. He had always focused and loved putting the message toward his life. But what did anything else really matter right now? He'd lost his son and couldn't even bury him. What could be worse than that?

—⁓—

Arianna sat alone in her bedroom on Christmas night, rocking in the chair she had bought while pregnant with Chase. She'd gained a total of forty-two pounds in her pregnancy, which caused back pain in the third trimester, so most of the rockers she had tested out were uncomfortable.

"I feel like the princess and the pea!" she'd laughed with Alan as they tried a dozen chairs at one store after another. It had been fun, albeit tiring, to create a baby registry and decorate a zoo-animal-themed nursery together.

"No kidding." He rolled his eyes teasingly.

It was at the sixth store where they finally purchased a green, soft, very cozy rocker.

"Perfect!" Arianna nestled into the cushions and didn't want to get up. Maybe she was just exhausted from shopping by that point, but it did turn out to be a great chair. She nursed Chase for nine months while sitting there, which were the most sacred of moments.

Now, she was alone in the darkness, aside from the lights blinking on a ceramic Christmas tree that sat on the windowsill.

Amy Grant was softly singing "Breath of Heaven" from the CD player. The song would always make Arianna think of Chase and that special night they'd had decorating the tree. How would she ever be able to take their Christmas decorations down?

The heavy wind outside caused the walls of the apartment to vibrate, and Arianna stared into the haze of snow through the window and wondered if her child was somewhere in the cold.

The thoughts that crossed Arianna's mind were too much to bear. Her mom thought she should see a counselor, but what did it matter? She didn't care about being happy anymore. How could she ever smile and laugh again, not knowing if her son was crying himself to sleep every night? Unless someone brought Chase home, she didn't really care if she did anything else in her life again.

As she rocked in the chair, she tightly clutched Chase's brown bear with the words *I Love You* inscribed on the tummy. If the cord on the bear's back was pulled, the melody "Twinkle Twinkle Little Star" played. It was Chase's favorite song.

She remembered how, at four months old, he'd started fighting bedtime. He had always fallen asleep anywhere, at anytime, until then. But, that summer, he didn't want to sleep alone in his crib. Arianna used to rub his back to soothe him and reassure him that he was okay, and she would always be there for him. He would still cry, though, until she began the sweet song. Almost immediately, his body relaxed under her palm, and his cries became softer and slower until he took a deep breath and was in a peaceful slumber. She carefully pulled her hand away before her tune became a whisper and then tip-toed out of his nursery.

Oh how she wished she could go into his bedroom right now and watch him sleep—see his tummy grow big and then fall back in, touch his tousled hair and brush it away from his heavy eyelids with long lashes, and kiss his full, pouty lips.

One night, when he was about eleven months old, she'd even picked him up at three o'clock in the morning just to hold him. She knew some mothers would have thought she was crazy to pick up a peacefully sleeping child—*what if he woke up? He might never sleep through the night again!* But that's not what happened; plus, she knew at the end of her life, she wasn't going to care if she'd missed sleep. Chase had started walking that month, so she knew that her days with her son as an infant were coming to an end. She had stopped to smell every rose in his life, which to her meant no regrets. She had also never been short on affection with her son. Every day he looked at her like he'd won the mom lottery. Chase knew he was loved.

"Do you want to come out and have some hot chocolate?" Alan asked softly as he peeked inside the doorway.

"I haven't eaten or hardly drank anything in four days," Arianna confessed.

Her husband frowned. "I haven't had much either, but we have to keep our heads above water. Chase needs us to stay strong for him."

Arianna turned her gaze back toward the window. Tears swam in her eyes.

"Do you think he's somewhere warm right now? What if that woman took him and then just left him somewhere by himself? What if he's shaking under a bridge somewhere? How do we find him, Alan?"

"We have to trust that God is protecting him right now. We have to keep praying for a miracle."

Arianna pulled a tissue from her pocket—something she kept in there at all times now—and dabbed her cheeks. She set the bear down on the rocker and followed her husband into the kitchen. She noticed that the fireplace was on. The room looked like it should be cozy, but to her it only felt empty.

Alan handed his wife a mug filled with cocoa. "Let's sit."

They relaxed on the couch in their tiny living room, and Alan grabbed Arianna's feet and began a light touch massage. Arianna felt so relaxed, so tranquil, when Alan's fingers traced her feet.

"Thank you," she said with a sigh of relief.

Three years ago, it had been Arianna who had comforted Alan when his parents had died.

They had just started their senior year at the University of Northern Iowa and were running together as they often did after their classes were over. They had stopped in Alan's dorm room to grab a jacket since the warm September day had turned into a chilly evening.

Both noticed the light blinking on his answering machine as they walked back toward the door.

"Eh, I guess I should see what this is." Alan had rolled his eyes, probably assuming that it was a telemarketer.

"Alan Tate, this is Lois from the University of Iowa hospital in Iowa City. Would you please call me back regarding your parents? Thank you."

Arianna's stomach dropped. "What is she talking about? Why would your parents be at the hospital?"

Alan shook his head as he played the message back and scribbled the phone number on a piece of paper. His hand twitched as he held the cordless telephone and listened to Lois explain that his parents were at the prominent hospital because they'd been in a serious car accident.

Alan insisted that Arianna stay put in Cedar Falls, but as soon as he left, she regretted not going. She couldn't concentrate on her homework, so she rented a movie from the front desk. It was a sad video, though, so she turned off the VHS in the middle and went to bed—praying for the hundredth time that Alan's parents were okay.

She had met them only a couple of times, but they had already told her how happy they were with their son's interest in her. Having their approval meant so much because she knew right away that she wanted to be a part of his family. She could picture her dad golfing with his father, and her mom cooking side-by-side with his mother in the kitchen, since their parents shared those same interests.

Except, it wasn't meant to be.

The next day Alan shuffled into Arianna's dorm room with glassy eyes. "They didn't make it."

She embraced her boyfriend and rubbed his head as they sat in silence on the couch.

Each day for the next month, she put a gift in his mailbox that she hoped would cheer him up. She knew he liked to go fishing on occasion, so the first idea was a mason jar filled with gummy worms. On the front, she put a sticker in the shape of a fishing pole with the words *Hooked on you.* Another day, she filled a box with all yellow items—a can of lemonade, a banana, a yellow notebook, pencil, sticky notes, lip balm, and lemon drops—and wrote across the lid "A Box of Sunshine."

In return, he had given her a bottle of Mountain Dew, her favorite pop, with one of the sticky notes stuck to the front that read, "Thanks for all you dew."

Her heart overflowed with love for him, and she admired the way that he conducted himself after his parents died. Their deaths had aged him. As an only child, there had been no one to help him with funeral preparations, but he didn't drop out of college and spiral into darkness. He took charge in all areas of his life.

"My parents spent twenty-one years preparing me to handle being on my own. The best thing I can do now is to show them that they did a good job," Alan told her.

Until then, nothing bad had ever happened to him. He considered his childhood and family ideal; he couldn't think of one complaint with his parents, and life had been smooth and easy.

He had proposed just a couple of months after the accident, on Thanksgiving in front of family at her parents' house—after they'd eaten turkey but before pie. Arianna had no hesitation with her answer. She prayed that if she lived her life with him, she would have his same ideal view of life, and someday her children would be able to say the same thing about her as a parent that he had said about his.

Alan had, in fact, been a good husband: devoted to her, honest, reliable, stable, and her best friend. They had never broken up—he'd never done or said anything that hurt her feelings . . . until that night.

"Are you sure you didn't walk away from Chase for longer than you say?"

Arianna pulled her feet away and quickly sat up, knocking one of the throw pillows to the floor. "What do you mean? I didn't walk away from him. And, the woman behind the cash register verified that she and I only spoke for a couple of minutes."

"I just can't visualize it. I can't understand how you could let him out of your sight long enough for him to disappear."

"I don't know what to tell you. I wasn't expecting him to get kidnapped!" Arianna yelled as she placed her mug on the table in front of her and stood up. She'd been relieved that the police officers hadn't suspected her of any involvement, as it seemed any missing child case these days immediately focused on foul play by the parents—but it actually felt worse to have her husband think that she was a bad mother. She already felt like it was her fault on her own.

"Calm down, I'm not blaming you," Alan said gently as he rose to his feet and reached for her.

"Oh really? You're not? Because it sure sounds like you are," Arianna said, taking a step back.

"I was just thinking out loud. I'm sorry."

"And I'm sorry I came in here. It's unbearable to be in this room, with you, without Chase. This place is too quiet. It's not right. I—I have to get out of here!"

Arianna ran to the closet and forcefully threw the contents out into the hallway as she searched for winter running gear. She hadn't run since she became pregnant with Chase but couldn't stand to be inside drinking hot chocolate by the fire when she didn't have a clue where her son was.

"Ari, come on, you can't go outside in this snowstorm."

She turned on him. "I thought it was admirable how you handled your parents' death three years ago, but now I wonder if there is something wrong with you. This is our *baby,* and you act like it's just a bump in the road for you. I'm sick of you being so perfect!"

"It's not at all just a bump in the road for me! This is the worst thing that I could ever have imagined to happen!" Alan raised his voice.

Arianna finished layering for her run. "Then me, in the snow, seems pretty small in comparison, doesn't it?"

Once she was outside, she raced down the street and then the next one, screaming, with tears pouring from her eyes and freezing on her cheeks. She knew her face would be red and raw for days, but she didn't care. The *not knowing,* the uncertainty, was driving her crazy. With more desperation than she had ever prayed in her life, she stopped and yelled to the sky, "Please God, *please!* I want nothing else in life! I'm begging you with every fiber of my being! Keep him safe and bring us together again!"

CHAPTER FOUR

Thursday, December 21, 1995

Alan stared at the display of fancy gloves, hats, and scarves at the mall and wondered if he should purchase one to give his wife for Christmas.

Arianna had made it clear that she didn't have a Christmas list because there was nothing she wanted. Except her son.

It had been exactly one year since the awful day that had changed their lives forever. Chase had simply vanished. There'd been no solid leads, and hardly anyone spoke about the missing toddler anymore. Maybe nobody wanted to be reminded that something so horrific had happened in the heartland. Flyers around Des Moines had become scarce already by spring.

It amazed Alan how life had gone on, seemingly unaware that his soul was tortured every day. He woke up every morning with a sense of dread. No matter what he did, he felt the loss of his son. He couldn't look at anything the same way. If he watched a comedy, he immediately felt guilty for laughing. His wife didn't watch TV at all anymore, except for *Touched by an Angel*.

Even church wasn't the same. He and Arianna used to hold hands during the service, clap with the worship band as they sang loudly, and often stayed afterward to mingle with other members over donuts and coffee.

For the past year, however, they had stood side-by-side, stoic, and singing quietly. They'd declined requests to join a small group or become involved in the other ways they had at the church they belonged to prior to moving to Des Moines. They hadn't even attended a service since October—it was the longest they'd ever gone. It'd started when both of them came down with a virus and then another, but now they were healthy, yet neither one had mentioned going back. Really, they didn't mention much about anything to each other anymore. Talking only made them feel more alive, and what was the point of feeling alive if they no longer had the most precious person they had ever met? Chase had been so innocent; he wouldn't have been able to understand why the parents that he trusted with his whole heart were no longer in his life. He'd certainly be traumatized forever after having his security ripped out from underneath him.

Alan and Arianna's minds wandered when they read the Bible, and the verses seemed like nothing more than words. They still prayed, still took notice of their blessings, and still kept the faith that their son would be found . . . but children changed so much from year to year. Did Chase even still look like his pictures?

Alan turned from the display and noticed the jewelry section. He hadn't purchased a piece of jewelry for his wife since her wedding ring. He had always liked that she was a simple girl. She didn't wear make-up or care about stylish clothes, but he could tell that she secretly liked jewelry. Even though she hardly wore any herself, he had a feeling it was because she just didn't want to spend the money. He always saw her face light up when she complimented rings, bracelets, and necklaces on other women.

Alan pointed to a simple heart-shaped necklace with a pink stone in the middle.

"May I see that one?"

The sales girl smiled and removed the item from inside the counter. "For your wife?"

Alan nodded as he studied the necklace. It was perfect for Arianna. "I'll take it."

"It's beautiful; she will love it. How long have you been married?"

"Three and a half years."

"Congratulations! Any kids?"

Alan's smile dropped as he reached into his pocket and pulled out his wallet. He avoided eye contact with the woman as he handed over his credit card and shook his head.

His wife would be horrified if she knew that's how he answered those who asked. She would have stared the salesperson right in the eyes and said, "Yes, I have a son. He'll be three in February."

But Alan hated talking about Chase with anyone, let alone strangers. Once people learned that his son was missing, their faces clouded with sorrow, fear, and even a bit of fascination at the rarity of meeting someone with such an experience—no doubt they'd go home and tell people, "Guess what?! I met a guy who had a son that was *kidnapped*!"

Nobody ever knew what to say. It was always awkward, for him as well, so he preferred to avoid the subject.

He took the sack, thanked the jeweler, and walked to the parking lot.

Just as he was getting into his car, he saw Officer Sparks walking past his parking space. It was the first time he'd seen him in a year.

"Hello." Alan gave a nod.

"Mr. Tate. How's it going?"

Alan shrugged. "No word on Chase."

Christopher Sparks nodded. "I'm so sorry. We get calls from time to time with people claiming to know what happened and I'm always hopeful. But they've turned out to be dead ends."

"Yeah. My wife calls the DCI every few months, but it's like he dropped off the face of the Earth."

"Don't give up, man. There was that kid—Steven Stayner—who was kidnapped back in the seventies and walked into a police station almost eight years later. It happens. Please tell your wife I wish you all the best this holiday season." He shook Alan's hand and continued walking into the mall.

Alan shut the car door behind him and turned on the ignition. He leaned his elbow against the window and rested his head against his knuckles. He didn't have the same adrenaline as a year ago. Was it better to tell himself that Chase was dead? Alan was emotionally exhausted. He had tried not to give up on his faith. It was one thing to walk the walk when he only had praise for the Lord, but the real test seemed to be whether he could do it during the worst year of his life. In his opinion, he was failing.

—m—

It was dark when Arianna drove home from the bank. She had gotten a job as a teller in March. After spending all of January and February cooped up in her apartment, not even showering most days, she'd applied to a popular branch. At first, it took every ounce of energy she had to pull herself out of bed to be at work on time. What she really wanted was to hear her son's voice instead of an alarm. To work for *him* all day. She already had her dream job. Though she had sulked about her lack of career in the first couple of months of pregnancy, she never felt she was wasting her college degree. Chase was completely fulfilling to her.

He'd been an early-riser, calling "Mama!" from his crib every morning. She was relieved that he had never tried to climb out;

she had heard the horror stories from other moms whose toddlers were injured in the attempt. Chase had loved his crib, and she had hoped to avoid buying a "big boy bed" for several more months.

It had been the same routine each day—she scooped him out, laid him on his changing table to put on a clean diaper (no, she hadn't started potty-training him yet and wasn't worried), took off his pajamas and slid on an outfit ("Where's your head? Where's your arms?" she sang as he giggled and squirmed his body parts through the holes), and then carried him to his high chair in the kitchen while he snacked on Cheerios as she made him oatmeal with brain-fortifying DHA.

For his first snowfall, she and Alan had zipped up Chase in a snowsuit that nearly swallowed him whole. Being the good-natured boy that he was, he sat still on a drift with his arms sticking straight out and his face peeking through the tight hood while his parents chuckled at the cuteness. They fantasized about someday all making a snowman together.

When the weather was nice, Arianna often took Chase to the apartment playground. She clapped for him as he climbed the stairs by himself, held his hand as they walked across the bridge, and caught him as he shot down the slide.

She had packed lunch, and they shared a picnic on the bench. He had a cute way of crossing his legs at the ankles every time he sat down. She chatted with him, and he smiled and nodded but was mostly quiet. His first word had been "Daddy" at fourteen months old and only a few other words had followed before he finally said her name at exactly eighteen months. *Pure joy.* She had been sitting on the couch when he crawled up to her, laid his head on her chest, and said, "Mama." Love filled her from head to toe.

It had now been a year since she last heard that sweet voice speak her name. She shivered and turned up the heat in her car. She hadn't been back to the coffee shop where she last saw Chase, and had busied herself with her job, as did Alan with his master's program. When he wasn't studying, grading papers, or making new lesson plans, he played video games, while she took on extra hours at the bank or slept. Most nights her sleep was disturbed by nightmares of faceless people dressed in black circling around her son while she fought them off.

She often awoke, drenched in sweat, from dreams that always started happy—she was back in time, holding hands with Chase at the coffee shop. She would whirl around just as the woman behind her was snatching her son.

"Stop!" she always yelled, tackling the woman to the floor. But the ground would fall through, and she'd find herself falling into darkness, reaching up for Chase but unable to grasp his hand.

On rare occasions, she would win. She'd kick the woman and send her flying through space. She'd pick up Chase and begin dancing—and the coffee shop would turn into a colorful flower garden with the most beautiful waterfall she'd ever seen. They'd dance through the flowers, giggling and giving each other butterfly kisses. When she woke up, she swore she had been touching his face.

"Do you have dreams with Chase?" she asked her husband once.

"I don't know. I never remember my dreams," was his response.

They hadn't gone on a date since Chase went missing. A few times she had started to ask Alan, but he always darted to his office before she could speak, so she had the impression that he wanted to be anywhere except with her.

She was surprised to see his car in the garage when she pulled into the second space.

They had started house-hunting in one of the suburbs over the summer, and moved to their first home in the fall. It was a 1,543 square foot tri-level with three bedrooms and two bathrooms. Arianna had cried when they left the apartment where

Chase had last lived with them, but she couldn't stand the chill of spending another day without him there.

"What are you doing home already?" Arianna asked her husband when she stepped inside the door.

Alan showed his wife the fast food bag he was carrying. "Dinner?"

Arianna hung up her coat in the closet and raised her eyebrows. "For real? You came home to eat fast food with me?"

Alan set plates on the table and pulled out the paper-wrapped hamburgers from the sacks.

"Actually, I have an early Christmas gift to give to you."

"I told you. I don't want to exchange presents this year."

It had taken a month for her to finally allow the Christmas decorations and tree to come down after her son disappeared. Her parents had been the ones to do it, saying, "We know it's hard to put away the presents for Chase, but you can still keep them out in his room for him to open when he comes home."

Arianna had stared into space, which was usual now. She was in a daze every single day. It was as if a fog was covering her, and she could feel it growing thicker and thicker, but there was nothing she could do about it.

"Mom, I used to love Christmas. It was my favorite holiday. Remember how we joked about my collection of nativity scenes? It wasn't intentional; I just loved them so much. We counted twenty in our house. I used to beg that we start decorating our house before Thanksgiving, but you wouldn't let me because you wanted to make sure that I didn't forget that holiday. Then, I'd spend the entire month of December making cookies and watching every Christmas movie there was. I think I was the only ten-year-old who made Christmas cards each year to send to everyone we knew. Mom, I can never be like that again. I hate this holiday now. I will never celebrate it again."

"Arianna, don't say that. Jesus is still the reason for the season—that is something you can count on to remain unchanged."

"I know. And I'll go to church to celebrate his birthday. But *I have* changed. There's no undoing it. I'm going to do something different on Christmas from now on."

"Like what?"

"Volunteer at a homeless shelter or do something helpful to take the focus off of me and instead put it on others. I really haven't done any service in my life. But I'm an adult now; I need to take the initiative because nobody's going to do it for me."

Arianna had been busy getting ready for a solid week of volunteering for the first time. Now she was caught off guard when her husband handed her a gold box with a red bow on top.

"I realize that our relationship hasn't been the same since Chase went missing, but I still love you and think you deserve a gift. You've been really strong, Ari."

It was the nicest thing he'd said to her all year. She struggled to swallow as she took the box. "You don't blame me anymore?"

Alan took off his glasses and rubbed his eyes. "Let's not talk about Chase right now, okay? I want this to be a happy moment."

Arianna's eyes narrowed, but when she took the lid off the box, she gasped. "Oh wow . . . it's beautiful! I can't believe you bought this for me."

Alan helped link the chain around the back of her neck.

"Thank you." Arianna leaned in and kissed her husband—something she hadn't done for most of the year, and so she realized that close moments didn't even feel comfortable anymore. They had gotten so used to avoiding each other that intimacy had become almost non-existent.

At first Alan returned the kiss, but then he pulled away. Her heart hurt.

She supposed if they'd had a long history, maybe they could take a break from each other like they had and pick back up, but instead they felt like roommates now rather than lovers. She didn't know how to start over with him.

Arianna frowned. "Alan, it's hard for me too. I see Chase's face in my mind whenever I experience anything pleasurable, and I immediately want to stop. But I miss us. I miss the foot rubs and the *thinking of you* baskets that we used to make for each other. I'm glad we're both home tonight. We should cuddle on the couch and watch a movie together. It's been so long since we did that. Maybe we should sign up for one of those marriage conferences that I keep hearing advertised on the radio."

Her husband shook his head and sat down at the table. "I don't think other people can solve our problems. We'll figure it out. To put it mildly, this was a rough year. But a new one starts in less than two weeks, so let's make it our resolution to spend more time together then." Alan took a bite of his hamburger. "I'm glad you like the necklace."

Arianna opened her mouth to speak, but no sound came out. She sat down at the table, and they ate the rest of their meal in silence, as usual.

Why can't our new year start tonight? she wanted to ask. It was the anniversary of when they'd lost Chase, but there was no lying in each other's arms on the couch to watch a movie after dinner or leaning on each other. She appreciated the necklace, but it didn't change their completely typical evening: Alan shut himself in his office while Arianna prepared for the next several days at the shelter.

Arianna hadn't just lost her son this year; she'd lost her husband too.

CHAPTER FIVE

Alan was a late bloomer. He hadn't gone to school dances while growing up, and the idea of being in a relationship when he was a teenager seemed overwhelming. He preferred reading and playing the trumpet in the school band. Girls seemed confusing and high maintenance.

His opinion changed when he met Arianna.

During an ice cream social at their church in the fall of 1990, they sat at the same table. He immediately noticed her smile. It was contagious. She seemed so happy. He was convinced that she (not the light bulbs) lit up the room as she chatted with her friends.

His opening line: "That looks good. What kind of ice cream is that?"

Her response: "Oh, it's a rare one. It's called . . . vanilla."

Alan loved Arianna's laugh, and by the end of the night, he didn't want to say goodbye. He had to see her again. Wanted to get to know who she really was, learn all about her, and to be the one to make her smile every day.

He asked her out to a theater performance at their college and, after a few dates, knew there would never be anyone else for him. Arianna had a soft and warm personality, and her eyes truly sparkled. He'd always been on the serious side. She was happy-go-lucky. They gave each other balance.

Alan's voice was measured when he called Arianna's father and asked for his permission to propose. Phillip paused on the other end of the line and then sounded like he was beaming.

"Wow. My little girl's all grown up, isn't she? You're a fine man, Alan Tate. I'd be happy to have you as my son-in-law."

Alan had missed Arianna's smile this past year. The spark within her had been completely extinguished once Chase was taken. Alan had grown accustomed to hearing her cry every night. When she wasn't crying, she walked around in sweatsuits with dark circles under her eyes. She snapped at him frequently—at everyone, really. People who met her now would think she was touchy and cold.

He knew there was probably something he should be doing better as her husband, but he didn't know what. Marriage hadn't come with an instruction manual, and he didn't have his parents around to offer advice. He always figured she wanted to be left alone, and so he let her have the bedroom (where she usually slept with Chase's bear), while he often played video games until he fell asleep on the couch.

He had hoped the necklace would show his wife that he cared, but although she had kept it on until bed that night, she still turned her back to him as soon as she'd lain down. It was the common way they fell asleep these days—just a mumble of a "goodnight" and then a quick "good morning" as they passed each other in the kitchen while grabbing a banana or bagel before they hurried to work.

Alan didn't know how to turn intimacy on again. Emotion wasn't something that could be forced—he had tried, but all he felt was dead inside. Had he closed himself off to all feelings after hurting so bad when Chase disappeared?

Arianna had expressed to him that she took it personally. It had nothing to do with her, though. Sometimes he wondered if he was punishing himself. He just didn't feel like a man anymore. Even though the kidnapping was out of his hands, he felt he had failed both his son and his wife by not putting his family together again. Throughout his life, Alan had felt pride with always having a clear head, but ever since Chase had vanished, he was confused all of the time. He didn't know what he should be feeling or thinking or doing. On the outside, it appeared he was standing strong, but inside he was just going through the motions of teaching and grad school. At least being able to provide gave him a sense of satisfaction—really, it was the only time he felt good. The more he worked, the faster the weeks went by. Life, and his marriage, would surely get better in time.

When Arianna was a teenager, she begged her parents to let her start dating. She was curious about boys and had a different crush each day, but Phillip and Gloria wouldn't allow it. Instead, her mom bought an array of dating and relationship books for her from the Christian bookstore. Gloria wanted Arianna to get healthy messages in line with the Bible rather than those portrayed most often in society.

So, aside from choir as her preferred extracurricular activity, Arianna's free time was spent thinking about the man that she would someday marry. She often imagined the Christmas season, walking hand in hand with her husband to a tree farm and picking out the perfect Fraser fir to take home. She smiled at thoughts of strapping the big, bulky tree to the top of their car and singing carols on the drive as she snuggled into her husband's shoulder.

Once they were home, she pictured laughing with the man she loved as they untangled strings of lights and hung them on the outside of the house. She'd make a wreath for her front door, and they would put a big blow-up snowman on the lawn—and it wouldn't fall down from the wind or be flat an hour later.

Then, once the sky grew dark, they'd kiss by the fireplace and fall asleep under a blanket in each other's arms.

Clearly, she'd had unrealistic expectations.

It wasn't like that in real life. She had thought they had plenty of time to get a real tree, so she hadn't been in a hurry during their first few years of marriage. Now, she wanted to get as far away from Christmas as she could. Her neighbors would have to get used to her house being the dark one on the street—there wouldn't be lighted reindeer, plastic candy canes on the sides of her driveway, or garland around the pillars in front of her house. And, as for holding hands, laughing, and making out with her husband—there was none of that these days. She had never felt as lonely by herself as she did married.

Had her crying turned him off? She knew it must be a shock to Alan to have married someone whose personality had changed drastically. She'd heard guys complain about girls being full of drama but had always held her head high, knowing that Alan wouldn't be able to say that about her. Now, she supposed, she was dramatic with her every breath.

"What you see is what you get," she had told him once. There were no skeletons in her closet or dark parts of her. She was transparent and carefree. Life had been good to her, and she was completely fulfilled by doting on her son and husband.

When Alan had been sick in college, she'd brought him a basket of chicken noodle soup, tissues, and cough drops. Nowadays if he had a virus, she left him alone. She felt bad that she had changed, but how could he listen to her sob night after night and sleep on the couch? Did he really expect her to still be the cheerful, smiley woman that she'd been before Chase was kidnapped? She would never apologize for grieving the loss of her son.

Her heart soared when Alan had given her the necklace. *He was going to let down his wall and let her back in!*

But he hadn't. He'd pulled away and rejected her. And, with Chase on her mind twenty-four-seven, she really didn't have the energy to fight it.

Friday, December 22, 1995

Arianna was in charge of making gift baskets with clothing and other necessities for little boys and girls at a downtown Des Moines shelter. She had organized boxes of donated items—diapers, wipes, formula, baby food, canned vegetables, shampoo, soap, lotion, and so forth—and her heart melted when she handed them out and saw looks of appreciation on the children's faces.

She had decided to donate some things of her own—Chase's old snowsuit and hats, mittens, and scarves, and a few of his books and toys. She took several deep breaths and bit her lip as she handed them over, but she was confident that it was what God wanted her to do.

"Tractors!" A toddler boy squealed when he opened the farm set that used to be Chase's. Arianna remembered how, even at seven months old and just starting to crawl, he had moved the tractors around on the floor properly, as if playing with toy vehicles was innate. At the time, she had chuckled to imagine him someday at four years old as the stereotypical boy making loud engine and horn noises as he pushed around cars and trucks.

Now, she didn't know whether she would have the opportunity to see him at that age or his face light up the way it always had when she took him anywhere fun—the zoo, the science center . . . She had once thought that children were selfish and unappreciative until taught otherwise, but that had not been her experience with Chase. He had always acted so surprised and full of joy, as though he couldn't believe his parents were going fun places *for him*.

Maybe she could help another child's face light up the same way.

Arianna was glad that she had made the decision to volunteer. For the first time all year, a little bit of the fog that had been consuming her started to lift. She finally felt a small amount of peace.

She made sandwiches and handed out food as well, deciding that she would volunteer there more than just during the week of Christmas. Families needed help year-round.

"You're that woman," Arianna heard a voice say from behind her as she was putting on her coat to leave. She turned around and saw a disheveled, gray-haired woman who was tearing pieces off a bread bun that she held in her hands.

"Pardon?"

"You had that boy who went missing."

Arianna's palms became sweaty. She nodded. The Tates weren't often recognized, which was fine, except it always made her wonder how observant everyone in the world really was—had numerous people seen Chase's picture and then walked by him on the street and never noticed?

"Did ya find him?"

Arianna shook her head.

"Sorry to hear that. My husband stole my kid forty years ago, so I know the feeling. Have you heard of Mothers of the Missing?"

"No. I haven't."

"We're a small group here. We try to help get the word out about missing children and also provide support to those going through it. Of course, most are like me—having lost children to an ex after a bitter custody arrangement—but why don't you join us sometime?"

Arianna wiped her palms on her jeans. "Oh, I don't know . . . when do you meet?"

"The third Saturday of every month at the Community Center in Valley Junction. At nine in the morning."

Arianna pondered the idea. She had gotten into a habit of withdrawing from everyone. It might help her spirits to be around those who could relate to what she was going through.

"Okay. All right . . . I'll give it a try."

She was drained from crying herself to sleep every night for the past year. There had to be an alternative. At one time, she was sure that her husband would be by her side whenever she needed his support, but she'd been wrong.

It was much simpler back in college. Even though it'd been a terrible tragedy when Alan's parents had died, it had brought them closer. Until then, their relationship had been puppy love. Sweet, smooth, and starry-eyed. After the car accident, the honeymoon phase—she supposed it was—ended. They made it through the next few months with even stronger and deeper feelings for each other. They had something real, something solid. It gave her confidence to move forward with Alan to marriage.

Except, three years later, the "for worse" part of their vows seemed to have pulled them apart.

CHAPTER SIX

Monday, December 25, 1995

After Arianna finished at the shelter and arrived home on Christmas night, her parents and brother stopped by the house to take her and Alan out to a late dinner.

"I really don't want to go anywhere. I told you, I'm celebrating Christmas alone from now on, in my own way."

"It's dinner, Ari. You have to eat, and we're simply joining you this evening," her father said, his eyes sharp.

"Fine."

She was aware that she had become reclusive throughout the year. She didn't leave her house unless it was for work or the store, and she hadn't made any friends since moving to the Des Moines area. Most noticeable, she had kept her distance from her parents.

Like her husband, she'd had a happy childhood and a close relationship with her mom and dad—but they had always been strict with her and much easier on their son, two years younger than Arianna. She adored her little brother, though, so she never held it against him that their parents seemed to have stars in their eyes when it came to Nicholas. While she was disciplined for any slight misbehavior, he seemed to do no wrong. He excelled and was popular all throughout elementary and high school—eventually becoming homecoming king, class president, and a baseball star. But, he'd struggled in college, so he dropped out and married his high school sweetheart. After bouncing from job to job for a couple of years, he and his wife took off one day to a suburb of Seattle. Until then, Arianna had considered herself to have a close sibling relationship with Nick—they'd grown up as best friends— but now he hardly acknowledged her. It took him a week after Chase went missing for him to call her.

"Where's Vanessa?" Arianna asked Nicholas, referring to his wife. It was the first time they'd seen each other in over a year.

Nick rubbed the teal stocking hat that he was wearing over his shaggy brown hair, as they all walked to the Sandersons' minivan. "Oh, the doctor didn't want her flying on a plane in her third trimester."

Arianna's stride came to an abrupt halt. She knew her face matched the color of the snow on the ground. "She's pregnant?"

Nicholas nodded as he climbed into the vehicle. "Yeah, we're having a boy. Due in February."

Arianna had never experienced what she thought was vertigo until that moment. *A boy? February?* Her voice was hoarse when she finally spoke.

"What?"

It was the first time Arianna had ever seen her parents look disapproving at their son. Her mother's careful words did little to comfort her.

"We thought he already told you. Your father and I didn't bring it up because we assumed you weren't talking about it with the baby's due date being the same week as Chase's birthday."

Is this some kind of sick joke?

Alan put his palm on Arianna's back and guided her to get into the minivan.

"It's okay," he whispered, his breath warm against her ear despite the cold temperature outside.

She chewed her lip and shook her head. *No. It's not.*

Arianna was quiet on the ride and throughout the meal at the restaurant. She hardly ate a bite, and shredded her paper napkin on her lap. It seemed that each minute her blood boiled hotter inside of her.

Nicholas carried on about his fantastic new job as a contractor for a military company and described how Vanessa was going to start a hair salon out of her home so that she could stay at home with their baby *and* get paid. She was always changing her hair color with the season.

Every now and then, Arianna noticed her parents glancing at her, their jaws tense. She could tell they were worried, as she was not trying to cover up the glare she gave her brother. Her mother and father had always been able to read her well.

At what point had Nicholas lost his sensitivity? His sympathy? His compassion?

Memories flooded her mind of their childhood together. They were always giggling as they played on the Slip 'n Slide during the summers. They laughed as they ran through the cornfields behind their home to collect kernels that were on the ground to make a "stew" with leaves, grass, and rocks. Indoors, they played hide-and-go-seek and, on Friday nights with their parents, board games while eating pizza and drinking Coca Cola.

Every morning they walked to school together and every afternoon walked home. They shared stories of their teachers and their friends, and complimented each other when they earned good grades. They'd always had completely opposite interests, so they supported each other on their strengths and weaknesses.

One winter, Nicholas found a large cylinder lid lying in the snow.

"Awesome! I'm going to sled down that hill!" He pointed to a tall, snow-covered mound between the trees.

"No, Nick. Mom and Dad told you that we're not supposed to ever go down that one."

"Oh you're such a goody-two-shoes, always doing everything they say."

"That hill is dangerous!"

"It's not any more dangerous than where we usually sled!"

"Whatever. Suit yourself."

Her brother was eleven and thought he knew it all. She sat down in her pink snowpants and began drawing a heart in the snow with this week's crush's name inside. She was putting the finishing touches with the arrow through the middle when Nicholas screamed.

Arianna gasped at the same time that her head jerked up. Her brother's body was pinned against one of the trees.

"Nick!" Fear burst through Arianna's chest. She ran toward him, but the snow was turning red faster than she could reach him.

Nicholas had been "her baby" when he was born, and it broke her heart to see him in pain. She'd always looked up to him despite his being younger. He was always so confident and fearless.

She turned around to run in the opposite direction, yelling over her shoulder, "I'm going to go get help!"

Arianna sprinted as fast as she could to her house. She nearly tumbled down the stairs of her basement.

Her mother was doing the laundry. "What on earth, Ari?"

"Nicholas!" was all Arianna could get out. She was breathing heavily and kept seeing red snow when she closed her eyes.

Her mom dropped the laundry basket from her hands and grabbed Arianna's shoulders. "What about him? Tell me what happened!"

Nick was unconscious by the time the paramedics arrived. He had to spend the next week in the hospital with a laceration to his head and bruised spleen—but otherwise he was okay.

It had changed Arianna, though. Most sisters were preoccupied with their own lives in high school, but Arianna went to every sports event of his, helped him with his homework many nights, and even asked a girl to go to his first homecoming dance for him.

But it didn't go both ways. Nicholas had never shown an interest in what was going on in her life, and now he appeared to put her in the same category he would an acquaintance.

"When were you going to tell me? Once the baby was born?" Arianna finally spoke as they pulled back into her driveway.

Nick peeked over his shoulder from where he was sitting in the passenger seat, as their father put the minivan in the park position. "Hey, it's nothing personal. Vanessa and I didn't make a big announcement. We didn't tell Mom and Dad till the end of September."

"Right. Nothing personal. I'm no one special . . . just your sister. Did it ever occur to you that your son is going to be my nephew? That I might want to be involved in his life? No, probably not, because you didn't take much of an interest in your own nephew. You haven't been there at all for me this year."

"Arianna." Her mother inhaled and then appeared to hold her breath.

Alan placed his hand on his wife's knee and gestured for her to open the door to get out.

"Do you know what? It's fine. I don't want to be a part of you or your son's life anyway. I will be much happier if you don't ever talk to me again."

She exited the van and was blinded by tears the moment she set foot in her home. Alan followed a couple of minutes later. Arianna guessed that his delay was caused by apologizing for her behavior, which made her fume even more. Maybe they should all just go off and live happily ever after while she lived alone. She couldn't stand anyone anymore.

"I understand you're angry at your brother, but I think you could have phrased that better." Alan winced.

"You're taking Nick's side?"

"No, I agree, he had a pretty lousy way of announcing the news. But I don't think that he's intentionally been avoiding you. He probably just put off telling you because he knew it might hurt."

"It doesn't hurt me that he's having a baby. What hurts is that I thought we had an ideal sibling relationship, but yet I'm the last to know about such a big deal in his life. Clearly, I've really never meant that much to him."

"Of course you mean something to him. You're his only sibling."

Arianna shook her head. "I can't forgive him right now. It took him a week to call after Chase was abducted, he never offered to help, and he never called me again."

"So is this about his delay in telling you about Vanessa's pregnancy, or how he responded after Chase?"

"Both, I guess. I don't know, Alan." Arianna swiped her arm across the kitchen counter, knocking down a pile of mail and a box of tools they'd been meaning to take out to the garage. She yelled over the crash of the metal hitting the tile. "I'm so angry! I'm mad all of the time. At everyone!" She closed her eyes and pressed a hand to her forehead. "Including God. I haven't had the desire to read my Bible in several months, and I feel such distance with Him but yet no motivation to try and grow closer." Arianna opened her eyes. "I hate feeling like this. I used to be such a happy person. But every day for over a year, I have been seething. I'm filled with such hatred toward everyone that crosses my path. It seems no matter what someone says to me, it bothers me. I'm so alone! Nobody is there for me."

"That's not true. Sometimes I think you want to be angry, Ari, because then you won't feel sad. But it'll tear you up inside."

"Oh, thank you for those words of wisdom." Her sarcasm seemed laced with venom. "Alan, my son was *stolen* from me. I don't understand how you've been able to encourage everyone to just trust it'll all work out okay. And yet, you won't touch me because you blame me."

Alan stared at the mess on the kitchen floor. "No. I've never felt so lost as this past year. I want to be strong, but I've struggled daily. I can't seem to pick up my Bible, either. For me, it's not anger that consumes me but rather . . . being inadequate and out of control. Even though I know that it's not logical, I wasn't able to protect my son that day, and I haven't been able to bring him home. How can I be a good husband to you if I'm not a good man?"

Arianna kicked a screw that was rolling toward her foot. "Of course you're a good man," she said, ashamed of herself. "I had no idea you felt that way. All year, I thought I've been on my own with this—like, it's my problem and I need to get over it. We're supposed to be partners, but we haven't been."

"It was never my intention for you to feel like that."

Arianna pressed her back into the wall and slid down to sit. "I know that I haven't been the best wife this year. My brother is just one of many people that I've lashed out at. I never used to want to hurt others' feelings. Now, I'm almost begging for people to hate me. You want to know something? I don't care if everyone around me leaves, because I already lost the most important person in my life.

"We never even heard him speak his own name. Do you realize that even if he was found tomorrow, he wouldn't remember us?" She paused to allow a memory in. "He'd have no memory of the toy I bought him at the store on the morning he disappeared. He was so excited for a soft, fuzzy ball that he saw on a store counter in the mall. A ball, of all things! And it was bright orange! As soon as I paid for it, he grabbed hold of it and didn't let go." Arianna glanced at Alan. "You know, nobody ever found that ball. I think he was playing with it when he was taken."

Alan crossed his arms and sat down next to her. "So then he had fun right up until that last moment. Those two years did mean something. Even if he doesn't have any memories anymore, I've heard the first couple of years are actually the most important in a person's life. He was given the best possible start in this world."

"I know we're never promised that our children will be here until the day we die," Arianna's gaze fell to the floor. "They're on loan to us from God. But now that I know exactly what that feels like, why would I ever want to have another child?"

CHAPTER SEVEN

Tuesday, December 21, 1999

CeCe raised her hands toward her mother. "Baby up?"

Arianna lifted her one-year-old daughter off the ground and kissed the top of her head. The little girl was her clone when it came to looks—the same dark hair and eyes, and tall, lean body. CeCe's spunky personality kept both Alan and Arianna on their toes.

It was a change of pace for Arianna to be a stay-at-home mom again after being promoted to teller operations specialist in 1996, assistant manager in 1997, and then credit product analyst in 1998.

She was twenty-eight years old when CeCe was born in December of 1998. The pregnancy and delivery had been much easier than with Chase (she'd gained ten fewer pounds, and there was no shoulder dystocia this time, despite CeCe being roughly the size Chase had been), but the months that followed had been more of a challenge. CeCe was independent and strong-willed from the start. Being a mother again was a completely new and different experience for Arianna than it had been five and six years ago.

Unlike Chase, who had never minded being held by anyone as an infant, CeCe wanted her mother only. She was loud and feisty and screamed at the top of her lungs if anyone else picked her up.

How ironic, Arianna often thought. If this had been Chase's personality, he never would have been snatched from beside her so quietly, without her noticing.

It helped her to appreciate the hard days. Every time CeCe threw a temper tantrum, Arianna reminded herself that the spunk her little girl possessed would help keep her safe, even well into adulthood. CeCe was confident without an ounce of shyness and already had definite opinions.

At the same time, CeCe was full of the sweetest spirit. She already loved dolls and had a gentle way of taking care of them. If she saw a real baby crying, she would rub its head and offer a pacifier. Arianna was proud that her daughter already showed empathy. She was observant and smart (already speaking two words at a time) and had a fantastic sense of humor. She made her parents laugh constantly with her antics—putting Tupperware bowls on her head like hats and then walking around as though everyone wore them; pressing her face against the sliding glass door so that all her parents saw from the other side were CeCe's scrunched up lips and nose; hiding in their bedroom closet—her chubby little legs peeking out from underneath their hung clothes; and walking around wearing their shoes that looked massive next to her small body. Everything she did was full of so much energy and animation. Arianna enjoyed time with her daughter at bounce places and anywhere else that was physical and allowed CeCe to keep moving—as she'd been walking since eight-and-a-half months.

CeCe didn't replace Chase, but she did bring the joy of a child back into their lives. Arianna was happier than she'd been in years. CeCe was full of so much life and carried such an excited passion wherever she went that strangers couldn't help but smile and refer to CeCe as "Miss Personality" and "Sunshine."

Arianna hadn't planned on ever becoming a mother again. Having another child wasn't going to make what happened with Chase any less painful. And, how could anything compare to what she considered to be an ideal two years with her son? She didn't want to bring a child into this world with the burden of thinking her brother had been perfect in her parents' eyes; Arianna already knew what that was like with her brother (the tension between them still hadn't been resolved). It wouldn't be fair for a new child to be born due to her own brother being gone.

But, then came the day, a few months prior to the conception of CeCe, when she had thought she might be pregnant on accident. Her hands shook when she bought the home pregnancy test; what if it came out positive? Strangely, however, it was disappointment that filled Arianna's heart when the little window showed a negative result. Growing up, she had always pictured her adult self with more than one baby—Chase was never going to intentionally be an only child. Out of fear, she had changed her mind about having kids; she was scared to fail a new child the way she believed she'd failed Chase when she hadn't noticed him being taken from next to her.

"Satan would like nothing more than for what happened with Chase to stop us from bringing another child into this world," Alan had said more than once. "Fear would be the worst reason to not try again."

Arianna knew he was right. She had been ignoring God's nudge that it was time. She would have to be strong, but she could do it. Still, she had been relieved to know that she was carrying a girl, for at least it would be harder to compare that way.

It turned out that there was no comparison anyway, since there were no similarities. CeCe didn't even have the slightest wave in her hair, let alone Chase's signature curls. Even the toys and food and parenting advice had already changed. There were a few items like blankets that Arianna reused, but most of Chase's things had either been donated to the shelter or were kept in her walk-in bedroom closet, where she and her daughter now stood.

CeCe always screamed *louder* when Arianna sang "Twinkle Twinkle Little Star," so Chase's bear remained in Arianna's bed. There were still nights Arianna cried, still times that nightmares woke her up in a sweat, but she remembered why being a stay-at-home mom had been her passion—there was no greater sound than a child's laughter, no stress more energizing and revitalizing, and CeCe was the definition of love.

"Chase," the little girl said, pointing to a picture that Arianna pulled out from a box. They always kept a picture of Chase on the refrigerator, but she rotated the photos each month. CeCe had always known who her brother was. Arianna and Alan looked forward to having CeCe celebrate with them this February, as every year they continued to bake a birthday cake for Chase.

As Arianna carried both her son's photograph and her daughter back downstairs to the family room, she noticed the bare atmosphere and wondered, for a brief moment, if maybe they should put up a tree this year.

She still spent time volunteering at the shelter and had become an active participant with the Mothers of the Missing group as well. It had turned out to be the perfect organization for Arianna to join, as she actually felt like she was making progress toward finding her son for the first time in five years.

In the beginning, it had seemed many businesses preferred not to keep up posters of missing children. Maybe it was depressing to them, or even frightening. Arianna would drop off flyers with managers who acted more than willing to help get the faces seen, but when she returned days later, the bulletin boards were covered with ads instead.

The Mothers of the Missing group had helped her to get her story out. She had always been shy and introverted, yet she became a passionate public speaker in schools, kids' martial arts centers, and at many other events, including The Iowa State Fair and on Iowa Public Television. Slowly, she began seeing awareness again for missing children.

But, everyone knew to leave her alone during the holidays— that she was Scrooge when it came to joining in on any festivities. It had been five years since she sent out Christmas cards, decorated, baked cookies, or bought Christmas music. She still wanted none of it.

That is, until she saw CeCe's face light up at the mall yesterday when they passed the gigantic Christmas tree covered in big bows and white lights. Her heart broke a little when her daughter happily danced to Michael W. Smith's version of "Jingle Bells" while they shopped in the Christian bookstore.

Was she depriving her little girl of the happy traditions that she had grown up with?

No. Christmas is too commercialized. It's better not to get wrapped up in all of that.

"That one was always my favorite." Alan noticed the picture that Arianna put on the refrigerator of Chase in his stroller when he was about ten months old. The way that the sun reflected behind the camera gave the photo an artistic quality. His blue eyes appeared especially bright.

Arianna nodded at her husband, noticing that his own blue eyes had grown darker over the years.

Alan had completed grad school in December 1997. Arianna felt a little closer to him after that, once they began spending more time together again. But, their relationship still lacked the intimacy that they'd shared prior to Chase's abduction. Arianna felt as though their marriage consisted of just being co-parents of CeCe.

"I can't believe it's been five years."

"Neither can I." Arianna put CeCe in her high chair as the shrill sound of the timer announced that supper was done cooking.

"I still feel he's alive, Ari."

Arianna took a baking dish of lasagna out of the oven. "I always have."

"He'd almost be seven. Maybe he's in school somewhere. First grade. I loved first grade. My teacher was Mrs. Phyllis. I stuttered until I was in her class. It caused me to be quiet and keep to myself. But Mrs. Phyllis wouldn't have it. She knew I had potential and worked with me and a speech therapist each day until I stopped stuttering. I had so much more confidence after that. I made some of my best friends to this day. She was such a pivotal person in my life; I have no doubt she's why I became a teacher myself."

"Maybe Chase stutters too. I wonder what characteristics of the two of us he has. Does he enjoy math like me or history like you?"

"Or maybe neither. Maybe he'll be the starting running back for an NFL team."

Arianna gave a rare smile when talking about Chase. "I think nature might trump nurture in that area. We're both tall but built too skinny and with zero athletic ability."

"Hey, speak for yourself." Alan helped his wife with the plates and silverware. "You should have seen me on the fifth grade YMCA football team."

She snorted, but then her face fell. They were speaking of their son as if he was growing up in a normal family. If he was being raised by a kidnapper, he'd be lucky if he didn't turn to dealing drugs as his adult career.

They both said the blessing and then joined CeCe in devouring the lasagna.

After taking a drink, Arianna set the cup on the table and turned to Alan. "I received a Christmas letter from my brother and Vanessa today."

"Oh really?"

"Yeah. Apparently, they've just moved back to Iowa. It said now that they've had baby number three, they want to raise their children in the same area they grew up."

"Makes sense."

"I guess." Arianna pushed the food around on her plate with her fork. The situation with her brother still made her angry. One thing that hadn't improved with CeCe's birth was that Arianna was still consumed with bitterness. She had sent gifts for each of Nick's three children when they came into the world (Max, 1996; Jordan, 1997; and Sierra, 1999) to try to show that she really did want to be an aunt. Nick had politely sent thank you cards each time but made no effort to talk to her otherwise or meet CeCe when traveling to Iowa to visit their parents. She couldn't believe that he'd cut her out of his life as though they never had a history. It had taken only one bad moment in all of their life for him to dismiss her and make no attempt at repairing the relationship. There was nothing more she could do if he didn't want to forgive her.

"Do you think we'll ever meet the kids?" she said.

"I hope so. They're the only cousins CeCe's ever going to have."

What about Chase? Was he being raised with other children, or was he alone? Did he know what it was like to play and have fun? Did he have friends?

Arianna had a new optimism with the millennium coming, especially now that there was the Internet. Several websites featured Chase's picture (with an age-progression photo), and e-mail forwards went around cyberspace with his story. She had even bought a book on how to create her own website and completely devoted the site to her son. She spent hours a day at her desktop computer, learning html, reading the guestbook posts, changing pictures, and finding information about missing children to share. It was her regular routine during CeCe's naps and in the evenings and on weekends when her husband took his turn with one-on-one time with their daughter. Of course, that left little time for just the two of them—but she didn't fret about it anymore. Was romance really that important in the grand scheme of things? Her marriage wasn't awful, she told herself. After all, she'd never know what it was like to be abused—Alan was the opposite of possessive—and she'd not had to deal with other serious issues that couples faced. She and Alan didn't fight—CeCe wasn't exposed to screaming or name calling; rather, the child had looked with adoration at her parents when they were getting family pictures taken and the photographer told them to kiss.

Alan and Arianna had the same opinions on how to raise their daughter and agreed on practically everything from their political views to what color of paint looked best on the walls of their dining room. They chatted easily at the dinner table every evening, laughing together as they shared the same sense of humor. There was nothing Arianna had ever felt she couldn't talk about with her husband, and she knew he felt the same. She had no doubt that God brought them together to be married; this was who she was meant to be with for eternity. No marriage was perfect; so what if they didn't have passion? They paid their bills on time, had a roof over their heads, respected each other, and the shared emotional bond of having a son who was kidnapped. Aside from that terrible experience, there hadn't been many other stresses for their family to deal with. *Comfortable* described most of their days. No, Arianna wouldn't describe her marriage as "unhappy." Simply, Arianna and Alan had changed. They loved each other, but she supposed *in love* was something altogether different. Their relationship would never be the same as before the awful day at the coffee shop.

Arianna used up her prayers and her tears on Chase but felt happy when working on her website. She was convinced that Chase wasn't in Iowa. Maybe now, with wider coverage, someone would recognize him.

Arianna had wished the Amber Alert had been around when Chase was kidnapped, as well as the national talk shows that were regularly covering cases and featuring stories like his, but she tried not to dwell on the past and instead focus on the positive: her son was at an age now where he could come forward on his own!

CHAPTER EIGHT

That night after Alan and Arianna had brushed CeCe's teeth with her little Sesame Street toothbrush and non-fluoride toothpaste, put lotion and a sleeper on her, and read a book while she climbed from one lap to the other, Arianna's mom called.

"I know this is always a rough day. How are you?"

"CeCe's been a good distraction," Arianna admitted. "She doesn't know that it's the anniversary of Chase's disappearance, so I can't mope around too much. I did the laundry earlier and, while I was putting clothes in the washer, she decided to climb inside the dryer and peek out with the cutest smile. This might be the first year that I've laughed on this day."

"I'm really glad to hear that."

"At the same time, my heart still hurts for Chase. His absence is still felt even though we've been apart longer than we were ever together."

"That's perfectly okay," her mother said gently. "But your love for him is not reflected by how often you grieve the loss. It's okay to enjoy life even though he's not here."

"I know." Arianna did agree with the sentiment but still felt as though there was a tiny brick wall in front of her heart.

"I was also calling because Nick and his family are settled. They live in Williamsburg now. Please celebrate Christmas with us there this year."

"Oh, Mom. No, I couldn't do that. I'm not ready."

"This is the first year that your brother has lived in Iowa in seven years. You two really need to start talking again. You're family! It's ridiculous that you haven't even let me mention his name around you or update you on what is going on in his life. I refuse to keep this up any longer. Out of all people, I thought *you* would know how precious each day is with our loved ones—that we're never guaranteed another moment—and yet you've let this go on for *four* years."

"What do you mean that *I* have? Talk to *him*. The ball is in his court. I sent gifts when his children were born, but I can't say the same for him." Arianna was aware of the bitterness in her words but did not care.

"Have you apologized for your part? I've spoken to him and told him that he owes you an explanation and needs to move forward. You both need to get to know each other again now, as adults."

"What if I don't want to know him?"

"Arianna! Stop using Chase as an excuse not to be respectful."

Arianna's knuckles turned white as she continued to grip the phone. "Why does everything have to be about Chase? Maybe this situation between Nicholas and me would have happened regardless. As soon as he left home for college, I was out of sight, out of mind. Don't I have a right to my feelings?"

"Of course you do. But holding a grudge isn't good for your soul. Please consider celebrating Christmas with your brother this year."

Arianna told her mom that she'd think about it before she hung up the phone and took a shower. The warm water rushed through her waist-length hair and down the front of her face. She closed her eyes. The only images she could see were of CeCe hopping around and clapping to the Christmas music at the mall yesterday.

She sighed and scrubbed her face with facial cleanser.

The holiday had been different until now. For five years, it had been only Arianna and Alan. She'd convinced herself that CeCe wouldn't know life any differently from how they raised her and therefore wouldn't miss festivities at Christmastime. She had even imagined explaining everything to CeCe when she was older, telling her in a firm and matter-of-fact way that going to church and honoring Jesus on his birthday was enough. Arianna was so used to being abrupt to everyone and everything these days—it hadn't occurred to her until this year's Christmas season with CeCe that maybe she was being selfish. Would Chase want his sister to miss out because of him? Would he want his parents to? He'd had such joy the night they'd decorated the tree. CeCe was entitled to experience that same awe and amazement.

We do plenty of other fun things. CeCe has a happy life! I'm, otherwise, raising her the same as I was Chase!

Are you? A voice from inside her soul—one that she hadn't heard in a long time—pressed on her heart.

No, I'm not. Her shoulders dropped at the thought of not attending church in four years, aside from Christmas and Easter and a couple other Sundays in between. It wasn't that she'd stopped believing. In fact, she would be the first to call out that she was a Christian. Absolutely. It just always seemed like it took energy; with CeCe not sleeping through the night until recently, she and Alan were often tired.

Arianna rinsed the soap from her body and turned off the faucet. After she threw on a nightgown, she climbed into bed where Alan was already lying.

"Do you think I'm a good Christian example?" she asked her husband.

"What makes you ask that?"

"I don't know. I guess in the last twenty-four hours I've been questioning whether I am modeling positive behavior for CeCe." Arianna gazed up at the ceiling. "Until now, she hasn't been old enough to really notice what we say and do, but—I remember from Chase—she's going to start mimicking really soon. Am I an angry mother? I don't want to affect her in a negative way."

"With CeCe you're not angry. But, honestly, that's the only time I see you happy. You're still a great person and your morals are pure, but you do seem bitter most of the time."

Arianna sighed. "I have to protect our daughter, though. If we start celebrating Christmas again, like with my brother, are we just setting ourselves up to be hurt? Right now, CeCe is too young to care about a relationship with her uncle. But, in a couple of years, she will start expecting it and might take it personally if he blows us off again. After what we've been through in the past, my need to protect comes above all other territories as a mother. I really think it's best to just keep the holidays simple."

"What if I go?"

"What do you mean?" Arianna raised up on one elbow to look at Alan. "By yourself to my brother's house for Christmas?"

"Yeah." Alan took off his glasses and put them on his bedside table. He turned off the light and pulled up a blanket.

Arianna sat up and squinted in the dark. "That's ridiculous. Why would you do that?"

"Because I happen to miss Christmas. Plus, I like your parents, and it's important to them. I'd prefer to bring CeCe. What's the worst that can happen with her getting to celebrate the holiday?"

Arianna glared, but her husband had his eyes closed and couldn't see it. "I'm not ready, Alan."

"Sometimes the right thing to do is also the hardest."

"But how do I know if it's the right thing?" Arianna lay back down.

"You ask God. He will tell you."

"I haven't heard God speak to me in years."

What about the voice inside your heart ten minutes ago? Arianna bit her lip. God wasn't going to be bothered by this issue when there were bigger deals in the world—like Chase still missing. She pressed her eyelids together tightly.

All throughout the night, she rolled around, unable to get comfortable. She felt like her heart and her head were in a wrestling match. Was it right or wrong to put her family in a vulnerable position? Every time she started to make one decision, she immediately switched to the opposite viewpoint. She only ended up more frustrated, overwhelmed, and angrier. When she finally drifted off into a light slumber, Arianna saw the words *Proverbs 20:3* and *Romans 12:18.*

Having no idea what the verses were, she got up when the alarm went off in the morning and opened her Bible for the first time in years.

God says that it is an honor to avoid strife and that only fools quarrel. If possible, so far as it depends on you, live peaceably with all.

Arianna gasped. It couldn't be. So quickly? So obviously? God had spoken?

But that meant He was listening. That He'd been there all along, ready to offer help—she just hadn't asked, as though she could pretend that by not acknowledging her bitterness she didn't have a problem. She read the verses again, and a peace came over her.

"Wow, that is amazing. You haven't left me," she spoke quietly.

"Did you say something?" Alan rubbed his eyes, yawned, and climbed out of bed.

Arianna was sitting on the floor, feeling the weight of the Word. She turned to her husband and took a deep breath.

"Okay. It's going to be hard but I guess it wasn't a coincidence that there are more volunteers at the shelter this year

than ever before. I'm going to take off Christmas Eve. We'll go
. . . see my family."

Friday, December 24, 1999

There was a blanket of snow on the lawn when Alan pulled
into Nicholas and Vanessa's driveway. He prayed that everything
would go okay with his wife and brother-in-law. It pained him
to see Arianna hurt, and he wanted a resolution. He was a man
who typically avoided conflict, which was both a strength and
weakness. He got along with most everyone that way because he
wasn't easily bothered and didn't waste time on issues that led to
problems within relationships. On the other hand, he knew that
his marriage with Arianna had suffered because of this same trait.
He'd thought their lack of intimacy would have improved on its
own, but it hadn't. Maybe Arianna was used to it now since she
didn't mention their marriage much anymore. She spent hours
working on her website for Chase or tending to CeCe. Once their
daughter went to bed, Arianna sometimes sat down next to Alan
on the couch in front of the TV, but they didn't have the same
interest in shows, so within ten minutes one of them would get
up for the other television.

He missed her more than ever, but what could he do if she no
longer cared? He didn't want to draw attention to their problems
or upset her, so he remained silent.

Alan admired all that his wife had been doing within the
community since Chase disappeared, both with volunteering at
the shelter and with Mothers of the Missing. He had planned to
join her with service after he completed his master's program
two years ago, but he just hadn't gotten the motivation. He always promised himself "next season." Now at age twenty-nine,

he had hung up his hat when it came to video games and instead busied himself with coaching girls' track during the hours that he wasn't teaching.

He carried his daughter as they walked into Nicholas and Vanessa's home. A large Christmas tree was in the foyer. They were laughing at something their oldest two kids were doing, but their faces hardened when they saw Arianna.

Alan saw his wife's body tense for a moment but then relax as she walked over and gave her brother and sister-in-law a hug.

The couple seemed startled at first but embraced Arianna. Gloria stood off to the side, biting her lip, while Phillip snuck a handful of snack mix from a spread of appetizers on the dining room table.

"Merry Christmas," Arianna said softly.

"Merry Christmas." Nick nodded and then turned toward Alan to shake his hand.

CeCe had already run over to the pile of toys and was throwing balls around the floor. Two of the children were running around squealing, while a baby sat in an infant seat.

"That's Max . . . and Jordan . . . and Sierra." Nick laughed as he tried to point, amidst the chaos.

"That's CeCe, of course." Alan nodded toward his daughter.

"It's nice to meet you, cutie." Nick squatted down and smiled at CeCe.

"Please, hang up your coats and help yourself to the food!" Gloria clapped her hands together and hurried into the kitchen.

Alan couldn't help but imagine what it'd be like if Chase was in the same room with them, chasing his cousins and laughing. Alan's chest tightened as he hung up his coat on a hook and joined Phillip for snacks. Regular days were hard enough, but holidays made it even more obvious that there was someone special missing from his life. It was why, despite his continued love for

Christmas, that he hadn't pushed the subject with his wife to do more in the years prior.

"You have a nice home," Alan said to Nicholas and Vanessa. The house was a large, older two-story.

"Thank you," the couple said in unison. They were dressed in coordinating clothes—he was in a green shirt, and she wore red. The stereo was set to holiday classics, and it truly felt like Christmas in the room; Alan knew he resembled a giddy child. Having not celebrated for four years made him really appreciate the holiday family gathering again. He was so glad that his wife had changed her mind. He'd been filled with such adoration when he saw her reading from the Bible just like the old days.

What about you? When do you plan to pick up your Bible again? Have you really convinced yourself you are the same Christian that you used to be, when you've hardly attended church? He took a drink of eggnog.

Is it really necessary? Isn't it my heart that counts? Okay, so that's been a little different since Chase was kidnapped too. But you didn't make me to be lazy, Lord—I can't just sit back and expect you to do everything for me. It's my job to be a leader, and I can lead my life.

"Can we go somewhere and talk?" Alan heard Arianna ask Nick.

He saw the look of hope in his wife's eyes. It reminded him of the way her pupils used to shine when they were dating and first married. She was still in there, underneath the hard exterior that she now always possessed to those around her. But, she was fighting it . . . and he realized, deep in his heart, he was too.

CHAPTER NINE

"Yes. Sure," Nick replied, and he led Arianna upstairs to the guest room. A purple comforter was draped over a queen bed, with a chair and desk to its south, and a dresser to the east. A window on the west overlooked the roof. Nicholas sat down on the chair, so Arianna sat on the bed and took a deep breath.

"I owe you an apology, Nick. I'm sorry for what I said to you four years ago. I've been consumed by anger since Chase was abducted. It's no excuse, but it's a fact. Having another child has been softening my heart, but it's still a struggle. No matter how hard I try, I'm just so used to feeling bitter now. I know I need to make God a priority in my life again. I think that is my only key to letting it go."

Her brother leaned forward and put his head between us hands.

"You really hurt me with your words, Arianna. I can't condone it just because of what you've been going through."

Arianna shook her head. "I don't expect you to *condone* it. But I admit that I am disappointed that you can't forgive me after one argument in over two decades."

"It's more than that—"

Just then, Arianna's beeper went off. It was the Mothers of the Missing group.

"Excuse me. I need to make a phone call. I'd like to finish this conversation, though."

Nick stood up and gestured for her to go through the doorway first.

When she returned downstairs, she saw her husband raise his eyebrows. Arianna shook her head to let him know the issue with her brother hadn't been resolved.

"I just got paged from the Mothers of the Missing group. This never happens, so I need to see what it is."

"Oh, yes, go ahead." Her mom showed her where Nick and Vanessa's phone was.

"Hey, this is Arianna," she said once the call had been connected.

"Arianna! You're in Williamsburg, right?"

"Yes, I am."

"There's a sixteen-year-old girl who ran away with her boyfriend. The police just finished talking to her at the outlet mall. She's run away to that area numerous times, doesn't seem to be in danger, and is sixteen, so they told her to stay at her friend's house to cool off before her parents pick her up. But her family is worried she'll be gone by the time they arrive and will miss Christmas Eve."

"I'm on it," Arianna said without hesitation.

"Her name is Tabitha. Shoulder-length brown hair, freckles, was last seen wearing blue jeans and a white Hawkeyes sweatshirt. Her boyfriend has long, curly blond hair and a bunch of tattoos."

"What's going on?" Arianna's mother asked once she hung up the phone.

"A runaway here in Williamsburg. My group is pretty sure she's at the mall. I'm going to go talk to her."

"What about the police? Isn't that their job?"

"They already talked to her. Apparently she runs away regularly and isn't a stranger to law enforcement." She shrugged. "Her family will have to go to court if she doesn't come back on her own free will."

"That seems so dangerous, Ari."

"I'll have Alan come with." She glanced around for him, but he was nowhere to be seen.

"He went to go change CeCe's diaper in the bathroom."

Nick, who had been snacking nearby, pulled his keys from his pocket. "I'll take ya."

Vanessa, on the floor with her children, looked up in surprise, as did Phillip, who was watching TV from his chair.

"Oh. Okay." Arianna raised her eyebrows. "Thank you."

The outlet mall was just minutes from her brother's home.

"Do you do this sort of thing a lot?" Nick asked as they pulled into the parking lot and passed the golden arches of a burger place.

Arianna shook her head. "No, usually the police do this. We just help get the word out about missing people around the United States. But, if you were her parents, would it matter if she was unharmed and ran away often? No. Because you wouldn't know whether this would be the time that you never see her again. You'd keep fighting for her. You'd never stop."

Nick nodded and pulled into a parking space. They scanned the shoppers, but despite it being winter and Christmas Eve, there were too many bodies to tell who could be the runaway teen.

"Let's just start walking," she suggested.

They both put on their hats and gloves and headed up the sidewalk, scanning the faces of those who stood outside or by the store windows.

"You know, I admire you for all the good you've accomplished despite the tragedy with Chase. Mom and Dad have told me about the work you do at the shelter too. That's cool."

Arianna shrugged. "I don't like the idea of giving in to the devil. He wanted to take my baby away and destroy my life. I spent a year crying myself to sleep—and hardly sleeping—but since the first time I volunteered at the shelter, I have slept like I used to. Don't get me wrong; every day is still a challenge—there will always be a part of me that is missing and I don't understand why it happened—but there has been good to come out of the negative situation. I have been able to help others. We have a 'found safe' gallery on our Mothers of the Missing website with over two hundred recoveries."

"You might be able to add another one—Ari, is that them?"

Arianna caught sight of the group of teenagers that Nick was referring to. They were walking into a sub shop.

"I think you're right!" She grabbed her brother's arm and rushed in after the teens. All were wearing coats except for a girl in a white University of Iowa Hawkeyes sweatshirt.

Arianna stood back once they'd entered the fast food place. She assumed she wasn't going to be well received. She had come because the outlet mall was a public place and therefore could afford her some protection.

The teens began ordering sandwiches, but the Iowa fan stayed quiet, and her shoulders slouched forward. For someone who had run away, she didn't look as if she was enjoying her freedom.

"Tabitha?" Arianna asked gently.

The girl shot around, her eyes wide.

"Hi. My name is Arianna. Some friends of mine called and said your family is worried about you. It's okay to change your mind and go home."

Tabitha's face clouded. "I don't want to go home."

The boy standing next to her glared at Arianna. "The police have already talked to us. Leave her alone. She's staying with me."

"Yeah, stay out of it, chick!" another teen called.

"Is that what you want? Because now's your chance; you can leave with me."

Tabitha looked at her boyfriend and then down at her tennis shoes that were dripping with mud and melting snow.

"How about we just talk for a minute. Over there?" Arianna motioned to an empty table.

"Don't go with her," the boyfriend instructed, still glaring at Arianna. "Don't make this your business, or you'll be sorry."

Arianna shrunk away, knowing that he could have a knife or gun.

"Don't tell me what to do, Ross," Tabitha said.

The boy rolled his eyes, but the friend in front of him turned around and cursed at Ross to place his order.

Tabitha followed Arianna to the table while Nick stayed off to the side. She folded her arms and looked anything but approachable; however, Arianna reminded herself that she had chosen to follow her rather than stay in line.

"You're probably wondering how I knew that you were here. Well, I'm a part of a group called Mothers of the Missing in Des Moines. I had a son who was kidnapped before he was even two years old."

The girl's face was void of emotion.

"I hope that you never experience anything that awful in your life. And I hope that your parents don't either. I'm not sure who they are, if they're decent people, or if you've had a rotten childhood. But let me tell you, I know they love you, or else they wouldn't be on their way here right now because Christmas Eve isn't worth celebrating without their daughter. You have what— two years before you graduate high school? Don't quit now. Finish it out. If you want to take off across the country then, do it. But don't throw your life away for some boy. Now or ever."

"Tabitha, come on; we're outta here," one of the teenage boys bellowed as the group headed out the door.

"You comin'?" Ross asked, poking Tabitha in the shoulder.

Still expressionless, the young girl stood up and followed the group outside.

Arianna tilted her head at Nicholas and sighed. "That was too bad."

Her brother sat down in the booth across from her. "You've got some guts, though. What happened to my shy sister?"

She looked down at her lap. "Life often forces people to come out of their shell."

"I can relate to that. Life certainly threw me some curve balls." Nick looked down at his hands. "Did you know that I struggled with my faith once I left home and went to college?"

"No, I didn't." Arianna raised her gaze back toward her brother.

"Yeah. I had some rough years. I didn't want anyone to know, so I distanced myself from you. I didn't consider that it might hurt you. I thought that if I was in your life and you saw what a failure I'd become, that'd hurt you more."

"You've never been a failure, Nick."

"You were so proud of me in high school, and then I went to college, where I was a nobody. It took several years for me to get my feet back on the ground. Now I fully understand that I hurt you too. I apologize that I wasn't there for you when Chase disappeared."

"Wow. Thank you. Your apology means a lot to me. You didn't deserve the way I snapped at you the next Christmas, though. I will always regret that." Arianna paused, recalling their earlier conversation. "What did you mean when you said I hurt you far more than just my words?"

"You never tried to be a part of my and Vanessa's life. You never checked in to see how I was doing when I left college and moved to Seattle. You were getting married and having a baby. Mom and Dad were focused on you, and I just felt like I'd let everyone down."

Arianna reached across the table to lay a hand on her brother's arm. "Oh Nick, all I ever wanted was to be a part of your life. My earliest memory is of Mom and Dad coming home from the hospital with you wrapped in a blanket. You were my first example of unconditional love. I used to push you around in a diaper box. You were my first playmate." She gave his arm a gentle squeeze. "I felt so lucky to have you, and it scared me to death when you ran into that tree sixteen years ago. Remember that?" Nick nodded, and Arianna continued. "I'd never seen so much blood . . . and on white snow . . . I wanted to just hold you close forever, but I knew I couldn't. We had our own paths to take in life. I left home and— you're right—we both are guilty of being self-absorbed in our own little worlds with our own problems." She released his arm and leaned back, shaking her head. "We didn't reach out when we needed each other the most. We should have communicated; we shouldn't have kept these struggles to ourselves. But you have never let our family down. You've turned out wonderfully. I adore you as much now as I did when I used to call you Baby Nicky and rock you to sleep."

Nick grinned. "Thanks, Sis. I had no idea I meant so much to you. You mean just as much to me. I wish I hadn't waited to talk to you. I guess it's taken me this long to get myself and my life figured out. I want to know more about what Chase was like, I want to be an uncle to CeCe, and I want you to be involved in the lives of my children as well. I forgive you and accept your apology from earlier."

Arianna stood up, tears filling her eyes, and hugged her brother. "That means so much," she whispered in his ear.

Other people inside the sub shop looked at them awkwardly. They stifled smiles and pushed open the door to the parking lot.

Tabitha was sitting on a bench outside, crying. Arianna lifted a hand to her chest before stepping forward.

"Tabitha? What happened? Are you okay?"

The girl shook her head. "Ross got mad at me for talking to you after he told me not to. He said never to call him again. They just left me here!" she sobbed.

Arianna put her hand on the girl's back. "Hey, you seem like too strong a gal to need him."

"It wasn't him that I was running away for. It's my school. I'm bullied every day."

Arianna scrunched her face. "Oh. Yuck. That is rotten. What do your parents say?"

"They think it happens to everyone and that I just need to suck it up."

"Hmm. I'm going to have to disagree with that. My husband is a teacher, and they have a no-tolerance policy on bullying. What about having your parents talk to your principal? Or transferring to a new school?"

"I don't know. I didn't think that was an option."

"I bet your parents want you to be happy and will do what they can to help you if it means keeping you at home. I can stay with you till they get here and chat with them."

Tabitha looked skeptically at Arianna. "Do you really think that even if I went to a new school, I wouldn't just be bullied there too?"

"I don't know," Arianna responded truthfully. "But I do know that this is a short period of time in the grand scheme of your life and that what matters more are the years *after* high school. So, if you run away now and don't get your diploma, I think you're going to suffer a lot more as an adult. I think it's definitely worth a try. You may be surprised—you could end up with new friends that are loyal for life."

Arianna handed Tabitha a tissue for her eyes.

Tabitha sniffed as she wiped her cheeks. "How old would your son be now?"

"Six."

"Why would someone take him from you?"

"I don't know. I think it was a woman. Maybe she couldn't have kids. Maybe she saw my little boy and knew he was special. Wanted him for her own."

"Do you think you'll ever see him again?"

Arianna clasped her hands together. "I do believe that I will. When, though, I am not sure."

Tabitha looked as though she were about to start crying again. "That's terrible."

"It is. But you can help."

"How?"

"Promise me you won't ever run away again."

Tabitha fiddled with a loose string on her sleeve. She looked at Nick, standing off to the side, and then back to Arianna.

"Deal."

Twenty minutes later, Tabitha's parents arrived. They seemed like caring and devoted people as they embraced their daughter. Arianna was optimistic that Tabitha was going to be okay this time.

"That was pretty incredible how you talked to the girl like that. I think she would have spit on my face," Nick said with a laugh as they climbed into his car.

"Like I said before, I feel the best way to rebel against the devil—who I feel is to blame for the evil in this world, including the abduction of my son—is to be an instrument of God and help other families. But I realized this year that I hadn't been doing the same for myself. For five years, I have been avoiding the whole Christmas extravaganza because it reminded me of the last time I saw Chase. That's not strength. Strength would be continuing with the same traditions that I started to teach him because I thought they were special. I told myself that if I was ever going to participate again, it would be for CeCe. But that's not true. I am also doing it for me. Because this holiday fills my soul. What better way to celebrate Jesus' birthday than to take part in everything? Do you mind if we stop at the store? I noticed that you don't have your lights up or Christmas decorations since you just moved in. What if I bought some and we did that when we get back to your house? It'll be just like old times when we used to put out all of those nativity scenes!"

Nick reversed out of the parking space and smiled. "I think that'd be a great idea."

—␣m␣—

Alan was thrilled to see his wife beaming when she and Nicholas returned home. He was even more surprised to see boxes of lights and decorations overflowing from her arms.

"After we eat, we're getting to work!"

The *we* turned out to be Alan, Nick, and Phillip working—when it came to putting the lights up around the outside of the house—but he didn't complain. Everyone was having a good time.

During their meal, Arianna and Nick shared the story of Tabitha. Alan was relieved all had gone well, as he'd been taken aback when his in-laws told him that his wife was involving herself in a missing person's case. Arianna had grown so familiar with the subject over the years that he worried she could get in over her head. He was completely opposite, preferred to stay away from anything that so much as hinted at the words "missing person."

Phillip had carved a juicy ham, and nobody could get enough of Gloria's side dishes. She was most well known for her macaroni and corn casserole—it was gone within minutes.

Alan was happy to see Arianna and Vanessa laughing as they hung up a wreath, for they had never had much of a sisters-in-law relationship, but something had definitely shifted since his wife had returned home with Nick. The air wasn't as thick, and everyone seemed more relaxed. This week had really been a turning point in their lives.

As Alan walked into the kitchen for a drink, he heard the familiar "Breath of Heaven" song on the radio. It always had the same effect on him as it did his wife, as if God was reminding them that He knew what was going on in their lives and hadn't forgotten about Chase. Alan looked up at Arianna and saw an anxious expression cross her face. He knew that she was questioning again whether she was doing the right thing by enjoying the season.

He caught her gaze and smiled warmly. She nodded and took the basket she was holding and began setting up a nativity scene. Alan saw a tear roll down her cheeks when she held the baby Jesus, and he placed his glass on the table and joined her. He was just about to put his arm around his wife, but then Phillip and Nick came in from outside and announced that they were ready for the big reveal.

Arianna wiped her tear away with the back of her hand, and they walked to the front yard to see the great display. Carolers were meandering down the street, singing "The First Noel." Their voices sounded angelic in the background as the family admired the icicle lights on the house.

"Time to open presents!" the oldest child squealed.

"And then it'll be time for church." Gloria picked up her grandson.

Alan sang along as the carolers passed Nick and Vanessa's house. It was really Christmas again.

CHAPTER TEN

Tuesday, December 21, 2004

CeCe sang like an angel in the Christmas musical. Arianna had tears in her eyes as she proudly watched her six-year-old daughter. It reminded her of her own childhood when she enjoyed participating in Christmas pageants. There was a feeling of warmth within her soul as everyone gathered around to hear The Story. The costumes took her breath away, and the music always brought her closer to God.

Thank you, Lord, for not abandoning me these past ten years. It's taken me so long to be completely back on track with you and there is no greater feeling.

Even though she had been full-swing into the Christmas spirit for the past five years and wasn't carrying anger and bitterness around day-to-day anymore, the issues within her marriage had finally hit the breaking point, and the year she was thirty-four had almost been the end of her relationship with Alan.

Into the new millennium, she had gotten lost in the escape of her website. After a while, even the hours spent there could not hold her attention and fill the void left by her husband. Nor could getting a puppy in 2001, although they adored their golden retriever as the newest member of their family, and Jewel was definitely demanding.

Arianna became determined to put her marriage on a different path. For a while she had thought that she could accept being best friends, roommates, and co-parents with Alan. CeCe melted Arianna's heart daily with the pictures she drew for her, flowers she picked, and hugs and kisses she gave.

Be thankful I have someone who does that at all. That should be enough for me, Arianna told herself. It did help temporarily, it did distract her, but she also knew that it wasn't the same as attention from a mate. Someday CeCe was going to grow up and move away. Then what would be left of her marriage?

For the first two and a half years after their wedding, Arianna had bought lingerie, but soon she had traded dressing up for bed for flannel pajamas instead. However, she found herself stepping into the store again to buy nighttime clothes that she hoped would get her husband's attention.

They did, but not in the way Arianna expected.

"Wow. I wasn't expecting this. Why the . . . lace?" he asked after they had put CeCe to bed.

Arianna lifted a shoulder. "I thought you might like it."

He smiled. "Well, sure, but you don't need to dress like this."

As if it was ridiculous because they didn't make love daily? Or even weekly? Maybe it was supposed to be a compliment; Alan wasn't tempted by porn or scantily clad women as many men were. Arianna felt sure she would never have to worry about Alan cheating, because theirs was the opposite problem—maybe he needed his hormone levels tested. Except, hormones didn't excuse why he hadn't told her that she was beautiful in years.

Arianna was crushed by Alan's reaction. He turned back to work in their office, so she left him and stuffed the new undergarments into her bedroom drawer, her body heaving with quiet sobs. Jewel, their golden retriever, gave her an affectionate nudge.

Arianna rubbed the dog's back as she wondered what it would take for Alan to notice that she was a woman.

But she didn't give up. Arianna bought relationship books to read together, taped advice shows off the radio to listen to together, and watched talk shows about improving marriages. Every Sunday at church, along with her prayer to be reunited with Chase, she prayed that there would also be a miracle within her marriage.

In their early days, she had enjoyed making scrapbooks for Alan. He'd teased her when he found cut-up pictures of himself on the floor.

"This is creepy," he said, picking up a cropped photo of his head and studying it. "You're not mad at me, are you?"

Arianna laughed so hard that tears came to her eyes. "I promise, you'll like it when I'm done."

And he always had. She'd made him four scrapbooks before Chase was abducted with quotes like *I love you not only for what you are, but for what I am when I am with you* (Elizabeth Barrett Browning).

Even though scrapbooking was more popular now than ever before, she had buried her supplies in her closet years ago, because the last book she'd made was the first—and now only—for Chase.

She was looking through one of the scrapbooks that she'd given Alan when she saw a notecard with marriage advice from her bridal shower. A guest had written, *Have courage for the great sorrows of life and patience for the small ones; and when you have accomplished your daily tasks, go to sleep in peace. God is awake.* (Victor Hugo).

Arianna re-read the quote, realizing that she hadn't truly understood the words when she was twenty-two years old. It meant so much more now.

She stayed up that night until four in the morning, completing another scrapbook to give to Alan for Valentine's Day. She no longer saved their movie stubs or restaurant receipts, but there were birthday and holiday pictures, as well as CeCe's birth and milestones. She found cute captions that she cut out of magazines and glued onto the pages, and she had a collection of coordinating stickers from a local scrapbooking store.

They hadn't celebrated Valentine's Day since Chase was living with them. This year, it had been on a Saturday, so CeCe went to stay the weekend at her grandparents' house. Arianna decided to make filet mignon (including peppercorn mustard sauce, mashed potatoes, homemade rolls, and cooked carrots with brown sugar sprinkled on top). She shaved her legs, put on a tight red dress, fixed her hair into a bun of curls on top of her head, and spent more time with make-up than she ever had.

Across the table, she spread out a white satin cloth that had been a gift for their wedding that they had never used. On top, she placed two tall slender candles and set out her grandmother's expensive china as place settings. The lights were dim, and she turned on soft music from her stereo.

Arianna sighed. Maybe cynics were right when they said that it wasn't necessary to set aside a special day for love. She always agreed that couples should show love to each other every day— but she also believed that just as Christmas celebrated the birth of Jesus, so should there be a day to celebrate the birth of a couple's relationship. To emphasize the importance of love and romance. It wasn't necessary to exchange extravagant gifts; many times a simple gesture was the most symbolic.

That afternoon, before Alan had gone to the YMCA to play basketball with some other teachers from his school, she'd told him that *tonight* would be the most romantic night they'd ever shared. They hardly ever had date nights. (They had never hired a babysitter in CeCe's life. Arianna would always be an overprotective parent; that's just the way it was going to be.) Arianna hadn't been able to stop smiling as she waved goodbye to Alan and thought about her plans. After dinner, they would go ice skating. She hadn't been since she was seventeen and couldn't wait to hold his hand and spin under the stars, getting lost beneath the moon and forgetting the world. She wanted to share a kiss like they had when they first started dating.

"I haven't looked forward to something this much in a long time!" Arianna told Alan to make sure he arrived home promptly at five p.m. He laughed, waved back, and promised he would be on time.

Alan was two hours late. She'd called his cell phone at five-thirty, but it had gone straight to voicemail. Arianna's heart sank. When she brushed a hand over her damp eyelids, her knuckles turned black with mascara.

Why had she dared get her hopes up? Alan wasn't the type to plan romantic evenings—history had proven that—and so she took it upon herself. All she expected in return was that he be here to join her in one romantic fantasy.

Arianna took a few bites of the filet mignon but had no appetite. The food had grown cold a long time ago, and so she began putting everything in Tupperware containers in the refrigerator, although she was tempted to feed it to the golden retriever.

The garage door sent a vibration through the house. Alan was home. Arianna stiffened.

He stepped into the kitchen and glanced around. "Hi."

After she shut the last of the food in the fridge, Arianna turned to him and said coldly, "You promised you'd be home hours ago."

Alan's face paled and he scratched his head. "Oh, Arianna. I'm sorry. I completely forgot that it's Valentine's Day. The guys I was shooting hoops with are single, and I'm so used to you and I not celebrating."

"You don't even really like basketball!" Arianna clenched her hands. "Is that what you want? For us to spend the next seventy years not celebrating love? Not having any passion in our marriage? I've waited patiently." She stopped him before he could speak to defend himself. "Don't get me wrong. You've been a wonderful husband. You helped me to get over my anger and to remain strong during all that we've been through without Chase. You're an ideal father to CeCe, you help me around the house, you're still my favorite person in this entire world to talk to and be around . . . but, Alan . . . there's a part of our marriage that has always felt very empty."

"I know." He leaned against the wall and crossed his arms.

"We've talked about this a hundred times before, but you have never actually done anything about it. Do you want to stay married to me . . . or not?"

Alan's arms dropped to his side, and his mouth opened wide. "Of course I want to stay married to you! Where did that come from?"

"We need help. Let's go to that marriage conference that we've always talked about. It's going to be in Omaha, Nebraska, in March. We never take vacations—we can make it a road trip, a little weekend getaway."

He shook his head. "All of this self-help stuff hasn't gotten us anywhere."

Arianna pulled the clip from her hair and curls bounced against her shoulders. "Then I'm done. It's been an intimacy-free marriage for ten years. I can't do this anymore."

"Now wait a second. You're leaving because of Valentine's Day dinner?"

Arianna groaned. "No! This isn't because of one dinner. Call this the straw that finally broke the camel's back, or whatever that saying is. It's been a long time coming."

"Where are you going to go? What about CeCe? Just think about this before you walk out."

"I have thought about it. I've been trying to honor our vows. I've been praying for ten years that it wouldn't come to this. But I'm going to be a shell of a person pretty soon if I continue to stay in a marriage where my husband doesn't treat me any different than a roommate or friend. I'm thirty-four years old, I'm not getting any younger, and I want to be loved deeply."

"But, you know I love you," Alan ran his hand through his hair. "Why isn't that enough?"

Arianna stared at the clip in her hand. "I wish it was. More than anything, I wish just you saying it was enough—then I wouldn't have spent the last decade pining for something until my heart finally broke into a million pieces. I'm not sure we can ever put it back together."

Alan's jawline hardened. "Wow. All right. If that's how you feel, I'm not stopping you."

The clip landed on the table beside Alan's empty plate. "I wish you'd consider the conference, because I'm giving us three months. If nothing has improved in May when CeCe is out of preschool, I'll get my own apartment. I can get a job back at the bank."

"I don't believe what I'm hearing. I can't believe you're doing this."

"I've hurt for too long, Alan, please understand that. Life's too short to not be happy in a marriage."

"I'm sorry it's been so miserable for you," he said sarcastically.

"It hasn't been miserable. I just can't stand anymore to not have what I've been missing for ten years."

"But that's Chase! As long as Chase isn't here, I can never fulfill you."

Alan stormed passed her. Arianna sighed. Was he right? Was she destined to feel like this forever? She could, indeed, end up truly miserable if they separated. She couldn't imagine a life without Alan. He kept her calm and was always there to rescue her when she was in any sort of predicament—like when she'd gotten lost one night in the rough side of Des Moines. Arianna had been in a state of panic when she called her husband on the cell phone—which she was grateful they'd purchased a few months ago. He spoke soothingly to her as he got on the computer and used an aerial map to talk her through the streets and guide her home. His voice, his presence almost always kept her from being anxious. He rarely lost his temper and typically believed the best in her. He was continually encouraging, and Arianna had more confidence with herself when she was around him.

Alan shoveled their driveway in the winters, fixed household appliances when they broke, and even changed the light bulbs. *But I can do all of those things*, Arianna assured herself. She'd gone from her parents' home to her husband's, but that didn't mean she couldn't take care of herself. She could learn everything she needed to and get used to life on her own. Anyway, she had no choice; she'd lost hope in their marriage. Staying when she'd given up wasn't fair to Alan.

Speak to me, Lord, like you did with my brother five years ago. Let me know what I should do.

CHAPTER ELEVEN

Alan's favorite role was being CeCe's father. Like most men, he had been overjoyed to have a son. To have that only son snatched from his life made him feel like a child who'd been eating candy that was grabbed from his hands. He would always wonder what could have been, would always feel the unfairness of life—but being a parent to CeCe was special too. He didn't have a clue about how to put pigtails in or braid her hair before she was two and a half and insisted that her hair be put up each day. She instructed him, not Arianna, to paint her toenails. At three and a half, she invited him to play tea party—an experience he never would have imagined enjoying in years past but which turned out to be incredibly fun. And, he'd never even touched a *Barbie* doll until she was four and a half and asked, ever so nicely, if he would play Barbies. Of course he did.

He couldn't lose his daughter to divorce. To be able to see her only every other weekend? *No way.*

What else could he do, though?

He had berated himself months ago when Arianna caught him off guard with the lingerie she bought. It wasn't that he wasn't attracted to her, quite the opposite. He desired her more now than when they were college students fighting the temptation to spend the night together after their dates.

"We could just cuddle," she whispered as they kissed goodbye outside his dorm room door their senior year. They could—no one else would care—but Alan knew he wouldn't want to stop at cuddling. He had wanted all of her . . . but in the way God instructed was between husband and wife.

He had touched his forehead to hers. "I'd love nothing more. But, I believe in the saying, 'good things come to those who wait.' After our wedding, it will be bliss to cuddle for the rest of our lives," he told her.

Why hadn't it turned out like that? They didn't cuddle; they didn't spoon. Why hadn't he kept his word? Why did Alan find it so hard to express his feelings to his wife?

—⟞ⱲⱲ⟝—

In mid-May, the swimming pool opened. Arianna regretted never having taken Chase; there were no memories of twirling him around in the water or sticking floaties on his arms. So, she had joined the YMCA and took CeCe before she was even four months old.

CeCe loved the water. She was a natural and had no fear of jumping in, often to the horror of those around her. There were plenty of incidences when CeCe was only twenty months old when her parents hadn't been able to catch her in time and she'd gone completely under the surface. However, she popped right back up, ready for more.

The Tates had then enrolled her in swimming lessons and, by five years of age, CeCe swam as well as an adult.

In fact, Arianna usually stayed on a towel with a book while CeCe swam with her friends.

One of the fathers laid out his towel next to Arianna on the grass the first day the public pool opened for the summer. "Your daughter's a good swimmer."

Arianna looked up from reading. "Oh, thank you."

The man extended his hand. "I'm Austin. Paige's dad."

Arianna noticed his grip was firm but warm. His teeth were the whitest she'd ever seen for someone their age, as she guessed him to be thirty-four as well. Arianna wasn't sure of his hair color, for it had been shaved—although she assumed it was light brown like his goatee. He was tan and muscular and had a barbed wire tattoo around his bicep.

"I'm Arianna."

"I know." He grinned and then looked away bashfully.

She noticed that he wasn't wearing a wedding ring. She made hers more obvious as she switched the hand that held her book. Typically, it was just stay-at-home moms at the pool during the week days, so she suddenly felt insecure in her black, one-piece bathing suit.

"Hopefully Paige and CeCe will be in the same kindergarten grade class this year," he said, placing his palms behind himself and leaning back. "Paige keeps telling me that CeCe is her best friend from preschool."

Arianna smiled and nodded, turning back to her book.

"I'm sorry, I'm interrupting your reading, aren't I?"

"No, no," she said too quickly—immediately regretting that now she was giving him an opportunity to stay. She had a feeling that she shouldn't be talking to him. On the other hand, she told herself, there was nothing wrong with having a conversation with the parent of her daughter's best friend. It wasn't like Arianna was a bombshell nineteen-year-old—she was in her thirties, a mother, and had been off the market for twelve years. Even when she *had* been young and single, she hadn't been one to turn heads. Boys in school treated her like the girl next door. She had accepted long ago that she wasn't sexy by society's standards, and Alan's reaction (or lack of reaction) the past several years had supported that.

This man, who didn't have one single flaw as far as Arianna could tell, certainly wasn't hitting on her. It was probably just awkward to be the only dad in a group of women, and he didn't want to sit alone in silence day after day while the women all talked.

He looked relieved and smiled. "Good."

"Where do you live?" she asked, putting a bookmark in her book.

"Over there on Iverson Road." He motioned to the south a few blocks. "What about you?"

She gestured vaguely to the north.

"Do you stay at home with CeCe?"

Arianna nodded.

"I'm a personal trainer, so I work six days a week but take Tuesdays off."

"Oh really? That's great. I should exercise more."

"You look in good shape to me."

Arianna blushed and looked at the time on her cell phone.

"Oh, wow . . . it's time for my daughter and me to go. It was nice meeting you, though."

She gathered her belongings together so fast that she nearly stumbled over her feet. She threw on her sunglasses and hurried to the edge of the pool.

"CeCe, come on," she called. "Time to go."

Arianna turned back and saw Austin staring at her. She knew she shouldn't be happy about it, but she wasn't disappointed.

—m—

That night, Arianna took out her wedding video and put it in the VCR. She knew one of these days she should look into having it transferred to a DVD, for the VCR was probably on its last leg. She was glad that the video still worked; it had been awhile since she watched it.

"Do you want to join me?" she asked her husband hopefully. They hadn't gone to the marriage conference in March, but they had arranged one weekend a month for CeCe to spend with her grandparents so that they could have a date night. Arianna didn't think it had really helped—there was still no spark between her and Alan—but she hadn't left yet.

"Oh, that's right; I guess our anniversary is this month." He sat down on the couch next to her. He'd never watched the video in the past, and she was surprised that he was now; maybe there *had* been a little improvement.

"Can you believe it's been twelve years? Look at us, gazing into each other's eyes and committing ourselves to each other forever."

After the minister introduced them as husband and wife, they kissed before turning to smile at two hundred seated guests. They joined their family and friends at the reception, surrounded by colors of burgundy and silver, cut the cake—red velvet—and had their first dance.

Arianna remembered that by the time they were whisked into the limo, their mouths hurt from grinning for the hundreds of pictures, as well as thanking everyone for their compliments and well-wishes.

She had been exhausted as she lay her head against the window and closed her eyes.

You can't fall asleep early tonight, her mind chastised.

They had finally arrived to the moment they'd been waiting for—literally.

Alan had relaxed on the other end of the seat, looking at the full moon outside his window. His hand was propped underneath his chin, which was covered with blond stubble. Arianna scooted over and snuggled into him. He smiled and put his arm around her.

They were still quiet when they arrived at the hotel, tipped the driver, and were given the keys to their room. Brown carpet lined the hallway as they carried their suitcases from the lobby to the elevator. Once they were inside, they pushed the #3 button and stared at the bronze door as they rode up to the third floor.

Alan swiped his card into the slot for room 304. Rose petals were scattered across the bed. There was a fireplace framed by stone, a whirlpool tub, and a stereo that Arianna turned on to a love song music station.

"This is nice," Alan said appreciatively.

"It is." Arianna stared at her groom in his black tuxedo, his burgundy corsage wilting already, and reached toward him.

That day had been the most romantic of their lives, and that night there was nothing to be nervous of, no one to be jealous of or worried about being compared to, and no reason to fear being broken up with the next day. They belonged completely to each other.

As Alan's mouth met Arianna's, she thought she'd found her happily ever after.

How wrong she'd been. Life had definitely not been a fairytale.

"Let's listen to our wedding song," she suggested now, twelve years later.

Just like with Chase, Amy Grant was the artist whom they had danced to at their reception.

"Oh, I think I'm wedding-memoried out. Time to hit the hay." Alan stood up.

She'd asked too much. Had been so swept away with feeling the romance of nostalgia but, in one moment, it was gone.

"All right. Goodnight."

Arianna stood up and looked at her music collection anyway. Rather than their song—"I Will Remember You"—the old cassette tape began with "How Can We See That Far." She sat back down on the couch, listening to the lyrics about a bride and groom say-ing their promises by candlelight.

> *And when I woke you in the dead of night*
> *To hold my hands, push away the fright*
> *Life had come — a son*
> *How can we see that far?*

The words were so true—on their wedding day they hadn't been able to see their future: losing their son, struggling with their faith and relationships, being on the brink of divorce. When they were twenty-two, nothing had seemed like it would be too much for them. They were in love and, with love, they could get through anything.

Except, it hadn't worked like that.

Arianna's heart ached for the love story that hadn't been for them. She felt betrayed. She had gone about love and marriage the way she was supposed to, and yet here she was: done. All the books she'd read that promised if she waited until her wedding night, her sex life with her husband would be the most fulfill-ing and intimate possible—she'd like to burn them! Between getting pregnant so early on in her marriage and having Chase abducted two years later, she felt she had been denied what was rightfully hers.

She thought of Austin and the attractive way he had looked at her at the pool. If what she'd been taught about remaining pure until marriage was a lie, then maybe the opposite was true for extramarital sex. It was as if an adhesive bandage had been placed over her heart, and she caught herself smiling as she relived her conversation with Austin.

What was she doing? Who had she become? She grabbed her Bible.

CHAPTER TWELVE

Arianna took CeCe to the pool on Monday instead of Tuesday the following week.

"But *Mom*, I want to play with Paige, and she comes on only *Tuesdays*."

"This way you can meet new friends."

"I don't want to make new friends. I want Paige."

And so, for the next few weeks, Arianna and CeCe joined Austin and Paige at the swimming pool on Tuesdays. Arianna learned quite a bit about them, like how Austin had been married for four years to Paige's mother but had been divorced for the past two.

"Do you go to church?" she asked one day while their daughters took turns diving into the water.

"Uh, no."

"Why not?"

"I have issues with God."

"What kind of issues?"

Austin brushed dirt off his legs and looked away. "My sister died of cancer when I was little. It was a slow, painful death. She was only three. *Three.* Tell me why God would allow a completely innocent child to suffer for two years. I loved that girl more than anything. And she was just gone one day. Never had a chance. She sat and watched other people live life while her days were spent throwing up from chemo."

Arianna tasted a salty teardrop that had quickly fallen from her eyes. "Austin, I'm so sorry. There is no good explanation while we are here on Earth, but I firmly believe that it will all make sense some day."

He looked back toward her and raised his eyebrows before he chuckled sarcastically. "Yeah, see that's not enough for me. I'm here right now, so I want to know *now* what all of this suffering in my life has been for."

"It's a broken world. There's the devil. There's free will. I don't believe tragic situations are necessarily always God's doing."

"What do you know about tragic situations?"

Arianna lowered her head. She hadn't told him. It wasn't like her to keep quiet about Chase. Although CeCe had helped her become more social at the pool over the years, Arianna didn't have many friends because she included her son in almost every conversation. She knew it made people uncomfortable and put them at a distance . . . a habit from the earlier days. When Chase had been kidnapped, a part of her had closed off from everyone. Opening herself up and forming a close relationship with others meant putting herself in a situation where she might get hurt again. She didn't have parties or join groups—Arianna wasn't rude or cold anymore as she'd been years ago, but she didn't go out of her way to get to know people. She'd had enough pain for this lifetime.

Arianna fiddled with a loose string on her towel. "I had a son. Maybe I still do. He was abducted ten years ago. I'd say it's been a very tragic situation."

"Are you serious?" Austin's blue eyes resembled saucers.

"Yeah. His name was Chase. He was almost two at the time."

"Oh wow, Arianna. I'm an idiot." Austin put his hand on her knee.

Being touched was so foreign to her. But even though it was June now, she hadn't moved out yet. In all honesty, Arianna had been happier since meeting Paige's dad—going to the pool and having someone interested in talking to her every day was more pleasant than thinking about which apartment to sign a lease. He'd distracted her from her problems at home with Alan.

She moved her leg away; it was a feeling that she missed, and she now realized how vulnerable she was to this man whom she'd been spending time with at the pool.

"No. Just don't make assumptions about people."

He put his hand back on her knee. "Arianna, I know you're married. But I like you. A lot. Don't tell me that you don't feel it too."

She gasped. After being in denial these past few weeks, the truth was out there now. Yes, Arianna had a crush on him too. This time she didn't move away. She could tell that he wanted to kiss her, and for a moment she fantasized about kissing him back. It had been so long since she'd been truly kissed or felt any sort of passion. She had thought she was dead inside, but something had stirred within her.

Stop, Arianna. It's Alan that you wish you had this feeling with.

"I love my husband. I've never been with anyone else."

He looked at her as if she was an alien. "You haven't?"

She shook her head. "I was a virgin until my wedding night."

"What? No way! I don't get that. Why would you want to do that? Don't you feel you've missed out?"

"No. I think it's the most romantic idea in the world. We saved ourselves for each other and can never share that experience with anyone else." Arianna's face grew warm.

"And that actually worked for you?"

"What do you mean *worked*?"

"I mean, you've never been tempted?"

"I haven't been until now."

He smiled flirtatiously. "Until now?"

This is wrong.

She stood up and began folding her towel. "I'm afraid this is goodbye."

"What? Why?"

"You're right, I'm tempted by you, and there isn't any other option since I don't want to commit adultery."

She hollered for CeCe to get out of the water.

"Wait—I'm sorry. I crossed a line. I don't want it to end like this. We're friends."

"We can't be . . ."

She turned to CeCe who was running over with Paige. "Don't run. You'll slip and fall. Tell Paige goodbye."

"Goodbye!" CeCe called out in her typical bubbly voice as she and her mom headed toward the gate. This time, they didn't look back.

—〰—

Arianna was grouchy as the week went by. She was disappointed that threatening a separation hadn't led to progress. She desperately wanted Alan to give her a reason to stay, but he hadn't. She missed Austin. Or did she? She'd talked to him only six times, so maybe it wasn't Austin she missed so much as the way he made her feel. What did she really know about him? What did he know about her? She knew he could bench 345 pounds, but what thoughts kept him up at night? He knew she liked to read, but what were her favorite books, and why did they touch her heart?

She had prayed for a sign by May . . . was Austin the sign that there were other men out there for her? Was it time for a divorce?

God hates divorce.

There it was, the same voice that had spoken to her years before regarding her brother. It was the truth. Deep down inside, she knew that Austin was not right for her. He wasn't a believer. God wouldn't bring her a man while she was still in a relationship—He didn't *want* her to sin.

But she couldn't stop thinking about Paige's dad. Certainly, this meant Arianna should leave her marriage because then she wouldn't feel guilty; it wouldn't be infidelity. If she stayed any longer in her marriage, she was going to come unraveled. Did the Lord really want that? It would affect her in all areas of life—how could she be a good mom to CeCe?

At the same time, she felt pain in her heart at the thought of introducing divorce to her daughter. The six-year-old always had a grin on her face, had such zest for life—she could make any situation fun and entertaining. Other children seemed to flock to her because she was so warm and carefree. CeCe was oblivious to any problems going on in her parents' marriage—but this would rock her world. Would she lose her spunk?

Arianna had heard that, statistically, children from divorce had more emotional issues than those who grew up in a two-parent home. Besides, she didn't know how to be a single mom; her own mother and father had an easy marriage, so she kept the matters of her heart private from them. They had seemed to stress more about parenthood. But for Alan and Arianna, being a father and mother had been their niche. It was their spousal relationship that neither of them seemed to know how to navigate. Was it who they were individually—would it be like this with anyone? Or was it the way they operated together?

Arianna panicked at the thought of spending the rest of her life trapped in an unhappy marriage.

Volunteering at the women's shelter and attending meetings for the Mothers of the Missing served as distractions from Arianna's troubles. The group had thrown a party to celebrate the incredible miracle of Elizabeth Smart being found alive last year, nine months after being abducted from her house in Utah. Arianna was ecstatic by the news. Chase would be eleven now, and she had renewed hope of finding him.

She was passing out updated information on missing children at a booth during the town's Fourth of July celebration when she heard a familiar voice.

"Arianna."

It was Austin. Her heart skipped a beat. He was wearing a baseball hat, white shirt, and blue jeans. It was her favorite men's look.

"How are you?" he asked.

"I'm . . . good."

"I'm glad."

"What do you say we get a coffee after you're done here?"

Arianna hated the word *coffee*. She'd had no trouble giving it up, cold turkey, ten years ago.

"I don't drink coffee."

Austin grinned. "I don't either. I was just hoping to talk to you."

"About what?" Arianna pressed her hair behind her ear and waved to people in the distance that she knew from the pool.

"Whether you've changed your mind about being friends again?"

Arianna did want to be friends, but she was fooling herself if she thought it wasn't inappropriate. They hadn't snuck around, and they hadn't talked about anything that anyone at the pool would have thought unusual for two friends, but he was a male and she was a *married* female and she couldn't help but wonder if that's what the term "emotional affair" meant. She hadn't told Alan about Austin or how she'd looked forward to seeing him on Tuesdays to share their day-to-day feelings with each other. For twelve years Alan had been her only confidant, and she knew that was the way it should be. Most disastrous was that she was physically attracted to Austin *and* he had hit on her.

She blushed and shook her head. "No . . . I'm sorry."

"I see. Well . . . if you do ever change your mind, you're always free to drop by. Twenty-thirty Iverson Lane. But promise me one thing—either way—don't settle with your husband, okay? You deserve a fulfilling relationship." Arianna watched him turn and walk away.

CHAPTER THIRTEEN

Once the fireworks were over and CeCe was sound asleep in bed, Arianna cornered Alan in his office where he was grading papers for summer school.

"We need to talk."

"Uh-oh."

She sat down on the floor, pulled her tan knees up to her chest, and wrapped her arms around them. "I met a guy at the pool this summer."

Alan stopped breathing for a moment. Nervous tension filled his veins. He stared at his wife, not sure what she was about to say but praying that it wasn't what it sounded like.

"Nothing happened. But it could have."

Alan felt as if all the air had been squeezed from his lungs. "What do you mean?"

"I mean, that he was interested . . . and I was tempted."

"To have an *affair*?" He felt as if he'd been punched in the gut.

Arianna looked down at the floor and nodded. "I'm sorry, but I thought you should know. I don't want to feel this way."

"Okay then, *don't*. Seems pretty easy to me."

His tone angered her. "Is it? Is it easy when your husband has hardly touched you in ten years?"

Alan stared at his wife—and her long, smooth legs—and he knew that many men had probably been attracted to her over the years. He'd been lucky none had gotten their hooks in her, but it still hurt to hear that she'd considered being with someone else. Alan himself had never once been tempted to stray; there was only one woman who possessed his heart and body, one woman he would die for, who he would do anything for . . . well, if only he knew how. He clenched his teeth.

"I've done the best I can, Ari. I've given you all I can give. I was hoping that since you didn't move out in May that divorce was off the table, but clearly it's not, is it? Are you going to leave me for him?"

Arianna rested her head on her knees and sighed. "I don't want a divorce. And no way am I getting into any new relationship. You're the only man I've ever loved. I don't feel there could be anyone more right for me than you. But," she raised sad eyes to meet his gaze, "I think our marriage has run its course. I need to start a new life on my own. I'll move out tomorrow. You can keep Jewel since most places don't allow pets."

Her words pierced his heart. Arianna stood and left the room. It was really happening. Alan's entire life had fallen apart. Ten years ago he had it all and now, if it weren't for CeCe, he'd have nothing.

Alan jumped out of his chair and stomped into the garage, slamming the door behind him. He pressed the button for the overhead door to rise. He was going for a drive to clear his head.

He turned up the radio and barreled through the streets of Des Moines, gripping the steering wheel. Despite the fireworks ending an hour ago, more people seemed to be out than usual.

His stomach churned. *How could Arianna do this? After all we've been through!*

He was so angry that he didn't realize he was speeding until he saw red and blue lights in his rearview mirror.

Oh, great. Alan had made it to age thirty-four without getting a ticket. *But of course, why not. This was already a bad day—bring it on.*

He turned off the radio, rolled down his window, and leaned his forehead against the steering wheel. A few moments later, the officer was at his door.

"Wow, Mr. Tate? I haven't seen you in years, not since I ran into you outside the mall."

Alan raised his head and saw Officer Christopher Sparks. "Oh hey . . ."

"Is everything okay?"

"Yeah. No. Arianna and I had a fight. I just needed some air."

"I get it, man. But driving's not my suggestion for when you're mad. You'd feel worse if you hurt someone. It's been a long work day for me with the holiday, but I'm at the end of my shift, so I won't write you up if you promise me next time you'll go for a run or something instead."

"Thanks. I really appreciate that."

"You hungry? I was going to grab a bite."

"Actually, that sounds good."

"Okay, I gotta head back to the station, but I'll meet you at Denny's in twenty minutes?"

"I'll drive on over."

Alan took a deep breath as he looked in his rearview mirror and watched the officer return to the cop car. He shook his head at himself in disappointment. He had been awarded Teacher of the Year but wasn't even in the running for Husband of the Year. Tears that he hadn't cried in ten years saturated his cheeks.

"I can't do it anymore, Lord. I can't carry this load on my own another day. I am a broken, broken man."

The admission of not being perfect was like a knife in his gut. He'd spent a decade trying to be the voice of reason for everyone else except himself—but he needed it the most. He was flawed. He was weak. He was humbled.

Time doesn't heal, God heals.

"I surrender to you. I surrender everything."

He had watched Arianna do it five years before and had fooled his own soul into thinking he had followed suit. He'd been half way in and half way out with his spirituality, and tonight Alan understood the term *rock bottom*. There was no fight left in him. He was defeated . . . but it was the most freeing feeling he'd ever known. All of this time, he'd been trying to figure out life—but it wasn't his place to figure it out.

"I'm so sorry, God. I'm sorry for being so consumed with my broken heart that I haven't thought about what's breaking yours. I'm not your partner; I am your follower. I will act in such a way from this day forward."

Alan pulled back onto the road and wiped his face. Once he parked his car in the restaurant parking lot, he sat for a few moments in silence with the Lord, asking Him to take over and turn his life's messes into a miracle. He was tired of making excuses for himself—it was like when he used to be a runner. He never started off with the motivation to run, but after he did it, it became easier, and he looked forward to it each day. It was time to just dive in and give his all to the Lord.

"I promise that I will stop closing my ears to you. I will stop hiding my eyes."

Alan was rubbing the back of his neck when Officer Sparks arrived. Alan cleared his throat, took a deep breath, and they walked in together and sat down at a booth.

"So fill me in. What have you and Arianna been up to?" Christopher took off his hat.

"Well, we have a six-year-old daughter named CeCe. She'll be starting kindergarten this fall. She's always been mature for her age—and bright. Brings a lot of joy to our lives. She's a goof, so she makes us laugh every day. But Ari and me . . . we're not doing so well. She's planning to leave me tomorrow."

"Leave you? Like get a divorce?" The officer put down his menu. "Wow. I didn't see that coming at all. You didn't strike me as the divorce type. I guess it really can happen to anyone."

"We just never got it back after Chase disappeared."

"Got what back?"

"She wants passion, romance . . . all that stuff that I just don't have to give."

"Please tell me that's not the only reason."

"I think so; I mean everything else is good. I know, pretty crazy, huh?"

"Pretty crazy of *you* if you let her go."

"What do you mean? It's her choice."

Christopher paused when the waitress took their orders and then continued.

"I didn't used to think romance was a big deal, either. Poetry? Yeah, right. Mushy cards? Come on, I have football to watch. Candlelight dinner? I was born in the twentieth century—I prefer electricity. Dancing? *Please.* But the thing is, I married a woman who liked all of that. Her name was Jenna. We got married when we were twenty-four. Every year she asked me for flowers. That's it. She didn't nag me about much. Just wanted flowers sometimes. And I always thought, what's the big deal? Flowers die. They cost money, and they last a week. We got along, had a good marriage, there was so much more in the grand scheme of things—we didn't need that extra stuff.

"But those things *weren't* extra to her. She was so giddy when we were first married, always planning fun activities for us to do. Stuff I'd never think of—watching the fireworks on the Fourth of July from the back of my pick-up truck, having a picnic on a hill underneath the stars . . . She was an artist, so she used to make her own cards for me. I'd find them around the house, in my car, and in the lunches that she packed for me. They were sweet, and I thanked her, but I also told her that I didn't need her to do all that stuff for me. Kinda put pressure on me, ya know? I mean, I wasn't going to do the same for her, just wasn't natural for me.

"She was crushed. Truly crushed. She held back after that. She used to make cassette tapes of love songs for me, but she stopped. She had talked about taking one of those all-inclusive romantic beach vacations, but I told her I don't like to travel. I'm a homebody. Having my girl as my wife was all *I* needed. I couldn't see that it was her way of complimenting me. Out of all of the people in the world, I was the one she wanted to be with at all times. I was the one she was always thinking about and wanting to try new things with.

"I'll tell ya, our marriage changed. For me to think that stuff didn't matter and that our relationship wouldn't falter was just selfish. Maybe Arianna is like Jenna. Maybe they need feeling and emotion. And maybe you're like me—it's hard to express that in their way. It's not a problem when both people in the marriage want and don't want the same things. But it gets to be a problem when one does start wanting something and the other person doesn't or can't compromise for whatever reason. For me, it was pride. They say pride is the longest distance between two people. We argued more as the years went by, stopped spending as much time together . . . and so I wasn't with her when she went to an art show one night. It was winter . . . the roads were slick . . . she lost control and was killed in a car accident.

"She got her flowers from me, though. The first flowers I ever bought were for her funeral."

CHAPTER FOURTEEN

"Wow." Alan stared at the cop, feeling as though he'd been smacked on the head.

"It was so easy, man. Tell me why I couldn't have done that before? I just wanted to be in my comfort zone. Well, guess what? I haven't been comfortable since." He spread his hands wide. "That was thirteen years ago. There's been no woman who has come close to comparing to Jenna. I wish she could have known how much I appreciated her, how much I treasured her, and that I didn't take her for granted. She was worth putting forth the same time and energy that I put toward my job—and I told myself that all of the time, but it didn't matter because I didn't show her. It's too late for Jenna and me, but it's not for you."

The waitress brought their food, and Alan stared at his steak as he shook salt and pepper on top. His appetite had vanished.

"Starting romantic gestures now doesn't seem like it'd save our marriage." Alan grabbed his knife and cut a bite of steak.

"I agree, you should've been waterin' the garden from the beginning. Couples need to fight the urge to withdraw when there are bad things in life and instead come together as soon as it happens. It's okay to take a few days, but not weeks or months or years. People change, but the key is to change and grow together—not apart. Otherwise, you'll wake up one day and feel you're married to a stranger. It's something ya have to work on day in and day out, no matter how hard—even you guys right now. You haven't officially lost her to divorce yet, so that means it's *not* too late. You're a Christian man . . . don't you suppose it's the enemy that tells couples to put it off for later, and they think they can—but then one day, before they know it, their marriage really is over?"

Alan chewed his steak while he cut another piece, remembering how years ago he had told himself that marriage hadn't come with an instruction manual. But it had. Lately, when reading his Bible, he was stunned to notice that he hadn't been following God's Word of all that a husband should be to his wife. Corinthians had instructed him not to deprive his wife of intimacy. Romans 12:10 stated, "Above all things have intense and unfailing love for one another." John 3:18 said, "Let us stop just *saying* we love people; let us *really* love them, and *show it* by our *actions*."

Why had it taken him so long to realize that while he was trying to keep his faith during the storm of losing Chase, and being a good spiritual leader, he had neglected his wife?

Christopher Sparks hadn't been able to save Chase, but maybe he had saved Alan's marriage.

"You're right. I have to get back home to Arianna. Now."

When Alan walked into the house, he found his wife packing upstairs in their bedroom.

"All right. Let's do it," he said as he stood in the doorway. "The marriage conference. And counseling. And reading our Bible together every night. Date nights every month and something romantic every day. That's right—every day. It's been ten years. It's past time. I'm all in."

Arianna's face showed straight, angry lines. She rolled her eyes and continued to pack. "You're just saying that because I'm leaving tomorrow. I've suggested those things for years; that's an insult!"

Alan took a step toward her. "I get it now. I never believed before that the little things by themselves could make a difference, but I think all of them together could help us to have a strong marriage again. I'm really lucky that I haven't lost you yet, Ari. I think I kept trying to imagine us the way we were before Chase was abducted, and it seemed impossible. But the truth is, nobody has that forever, with or without losing a child. Everyone's relationship changes and goes through phases. That's just how it works; it's impossible to prevent. You don't go backward, you go forward. You find where you are today, and you *work* at staying in love. It's not a passive experience."

Arianna raised an eyebrow. "Where did you go when you left here? Who *are* you?"

Alan smiled apologetically and drew his wife to him, taking her hand in his. "I'm sorry it's taken me so long to tell you this, but I don't blame you for Chase's disappearance. I never have. I want a fresh start with you. From this moment on."

Alan pressed his lips to those of the only woman he'd ever been in love with. His kisses trailed down her neck and reached her heart before he lifted his head and gazed into her eyes. "I promise I will spend the rest of my life making sure this is exactly where your heart always wants to be."

—∞—

Alan kept his word. The next five months had been the best of their marriage. Amazingly, even better than their first two years (before Chase was abducted)—because now they appreciated and recognized all that they had missed with each other through the years. It was a miracle that the hardships had not torn apart their marriage. They treated each day as another chance to fall in love. It was a day-to-day priority for both of them to prevent their relationship from ever falling to the wayside again.

They became active participants in church for the first time in ten years, including joining a marriage small group. They held hands, sang, clapped, and gave the Lord their all. It reminded them of the way they'd been back in college, before life had shown them a nasty side. Their hearts had never felt so free and full of elation—it was the best feeling in the world. They went to the national Christian marriage conference in the fall and found it so inspiring that they planned to go back the following year.

"I can't believe I waited so long. That was one of the most fun weekends I've ever had," Alan told Arianna. She knew she would keep their workbooks and other souvenirs forever.

Every night by the fire, they read their Bible together and, gradually, Arianna realized she was in love with her husband again. No, there was no butterflies-in-the-stomach-adrenaline-rush as she'd experienced back in college, but she was still smitten.

Before the Christmas musical started, she ran to purchase a drink at the concession stand, and when she returned to her husband, she smiled at how cute he still was to her after fourteen years of knowing him. He needed a haircut, but she couldn't wait to run her fingers through his hair later at home. Arianna had no way to explain how they had let down their walls to be completely intimate again—other than to give all glory to God—and they had made a promise to sleep in the same bed every night. It made her sick to think that over the summer she had almost given all of this up when the best had been yet to come.

It hadn't been a lie, after all, that they would have the deepest of intimacy in the bedroom. It just hadn't come right away. It had taken awhile, but once they bridged the gap during their day-to-day routines, it was like uncovering a side of themselves they never knew existed. They both enjoyed intimacy more at thirty-four years of age and after twelve years of marriage than ever before.

Arianna was thankful every day that she hadn't contaminated her marriage by taking Austin up on his offer. She still saw him around, but she no longer felt an attraction to him. Alan made her heart flutter these days, and there wasn't room for anyone else. Austin seemed to understand; he had found someone else after the Fourth of July.

"Can I make another request?" Alan asked one night with an arm wrapped around his wife's body.

"Please."

With his free arm, he picked up the beat-up looking brown bear that was stuffed between the mattress and headboard. Only one eye remained on its face. "Will you stop sleeping with this thing?"

Arianna studied the bear and allowed her body to settle into her husband's embrace. His arms felt strong and protective around her. It was her favorite place to be. No walls stood between them anymore—a bulldozer had knocked a large one of hers down when Alan had finally said the words she'd always longed to hear: *I don't blame you. Chase's abduction wasn't your fault.* She didn't need the bear for comfort anymore.

"You're right. I should have put it away a long time ago."

She had recognized and apologized to Alan for her role in their loss of intimacy. Her daydreams about love as a teenager may have been a little on the extraordinary side, and as an adult she had often expected from her husband what she could have only received from Jesus Christ. Alan was human; he would continue to let her down as he had on Valentine's Day—but that was *a good thing,* because otherwise she might forget to keep her worship toward God. *He* was the only One who would never let her down.

If Alan was going to compromise and do things for her that didn't come naturally to him, then she could accept the man that

God had made him to be and focus on what they did have together rather than what they didn't. Just knowing that they were
both trying, and that they both cared, made the most difference.
She had never felt so close to Alan as she did now. It was a much
better home for Chase to return to.

The Tates had arranged for CeCe to go home with a friend
after the musical ended. Strolling to their SUV after the program,
Arianna found herself looking forward to both Alan and CeCe's
two-week winter break. Each year, their Christmas traditions
included making homemade ornaments, baking a birthday cake
for Jesus, reading the Christmas story together, driving around
to look at lights in the various neighborhoods, and—if there was
snow outside—creating a fort and snow angels. As Alan held the
door for her, Arianna slid into her seat and allowed her mind to
wander through memories of Christmases past.

"There's something I'd like us to do tomorrow," Alan said as he
climbed into the driver's seat and started the engine.

"What's that?" Arianna turned the vents toward her to warm
up from the freezing temperature outside.

"Go get a tree. A real one. A Fraser fir."

"You've always said you didn't want to. Too much money, too
much work."

"I guess I changed my mind. Well, I mean, not every year . . ."

Arianna laughed—the same giggle that she'd had when she
and Alan first met.

"That would be wonderful."

Spring 2014

Giant raindrops slammed into Arianna's windshield as
she drove to the shelter, where she worked full-time now. She

could hardly see in front of her and was glad that she had only a few more miles to go. The car was silent while she concentrated on the roads. CeCe was in the passenger seat, on spring break from school.

Arianna's daughter was fifteen now with maroon polish on her nails and matching lipstick. She was still as spunky as ever, but Arianna was proud of the teenage girl that CeCe had become. Her boldness, determination, and ambition had led to her being a great leader in her youth group and within the church. She had shown an interest in volunteering when she was only twelve years old. Every year since then, whenever possible, Arianna had brought the younger girl with her to the shelter. At school, CeCe's favorite subject was math. She hoped to follow in her mother's footsteps to become the financial analyst that Arianna had originally aspired to be.

They both relaxed once the car was parked safely in the lot. CeCe grabbed the umbrella in the backseat while her mom checked her reflection in the rearview mirror. Arianna was forty-four now. Her hair was cut to her chin with strands of gray. She wondered if she had more wrinkles than she would have if she hadn't lost Chase.

It had been nineteen years and three months since she'd seen her son. Her website was still active, and every year she spoke with her special agent at the DCI, but nobody knew what had become of Chase.

On the bright side, Alan had gone on and gotten his doctorate. They still made time for monthly date weekends, and (almost) every day did something romantic for each other—whether it was waking up to find a note on the mirror listing reasons why Alan liked Arianna, or one of their *thinking of you gifts*, such as a jar filled of Reese's Pieces with a note on front that said *I Love You*

To Pieces. The foot rubs, which had returned after a long absence, were appreciated most of all.

Meanwhile, Arianna's relationship with her brother was still strong, and CeCe was close to her three cousins.

"All right, you're working the food pantry today," Arianna told her daughter once they'd arrived inside of the building and set the drenched umbrella on the floor by the coat rack. "I'll meet you back there in a half an hour—first, I need to talk to Paula in the office."

"Okay, Mom. I'll see ya in a few." After CeCe hung up her coat, she went down one hall, while Arianna went down the other.

It turned out to be forty minutes, so Arianna was walking swiftly as she passed the lobby again and collided with a child.

"Oh my! I'm so sorry! I wasn't expecting such a little . . . boy . . ." her voice trailed off as her gaze focused on the toddler. The curly blond hair, the light skin, the big blue eyes. She blinked. *Chase?* She blinked again. The child was still there, staring at her, assessing whether he should start crying or not.

What is going on?

People who were walking by looked at her curiously.

For the first couple of years after her son's disappearance, Arianna had numerous anxiety attacks, thinking that she saw Chase on every street corner. She was well aware that her son would be twenty-one now, so this little boy obviously wasn't him . . . but he was the spitting image! She'd never seen anything like it in her life. Her breathing became shallow, and the room spun.

Standing in front of Arianna was her son from two decades before!

PART TWO

CHAPTER FIFTEEN

Wednesday, December 21, 1994

Lacey Ray was eight years old the first time she planned to leave her life and not come back. Her mom was about to get married, but Lacey refused to have a stepdad.

She left a note that read "push play" on top of her 1975 Mickey Mouse tape recorder. Minutes earlier, she had spoken into the hand-held microphone and told her family goodbye.

Just as she was ready to walk out the door, she heard her mother and soon-to-be-stepfather's voices become louder and clearer in the hallway of their Kansas City home. She darted into the coat closet and held her breath. She could see them through the crack in the door—her mother's red hair and Kevin's full beard.

"What's this?" Her mom bent down, and a moment later Lacey heard her own recorded voice.

"I'm leaving. Don't try to find me. Enjoy your new life together. Peace."

The adults laughed.

"Lacey! Pick up your tape recorder now!" her mother hollered.

The third grader lurched through the closet door with tears streaming down her cheeks. "No! I'm running away, and I'm not coming back!"

"Oh, stop it. Kevin and I are getting married, and that's that."

"Lacey, it's okay. Come here." Lydia Ray rounded the corner of the hallway and took her sister's hand.

Older by three years, Lydia had her mother's red hair and freckles. Both girls had green eyes, but Lacey's hair was a blondish brown like her father's had been.

Benjamin Ray had walked out when the girls were two and five. He chose drugs and alcohol over family, and they hadn't seen him since. Lacey had never known life with a father-figure, and that was just fine with her. But her mom thought otherwise.

"It'll be okay. Mom's happy," Lydia reassured her once they were back in the bedroom that they shared.

"What about me? I've never been happy!" Lacey yelled. "As soon as I'm old enough to move out, I'm gone!"

She kept her word. She left home at the age of seventeen and didn't come home for four years. She had inherited her father's tendency toward substance abuse but tried to clean up her life at age twenty-one. However, she was back to living on the streets at the age of twenty-three.

There was one silver lining, though. She met Reid that time around. He was so strong, so powerful; she felt so protected and safe when she was with him. For the first time in her life, she wanted to get married. But, even getting pregnant two years later wasn't enough to keep Reid around. She hadn't seen him since.

"Please, come live with me." Her sister had begged on the phone when Lacey called to announce her pregnancy. "I can help you with your baby."

"I am capable of taking care of it myself. I'm going to turn my life around, Lydia. I really am."

That was the last time she'd spoken to her sister. She had a miscarriage and never got her act together. Now, two years later, she was twenty-seven and so tired. So hungry. So depressed.

Should she go home for Christmas this year? Lydia and her family lived in a small town in Colorado. Lacey imagined her sister and her husband kissing under the mistletoe as their children, dressed in plaid with their hair styled, stood by and smiled adoringly.

Disgusting. She wouldn't eat apple pie with them if someone paid her.

It would be nice to have a child at Christmas, though. People wouldn't put her down like they always did. Right now, nobody believed that she would ever amount to anything on her own. They always took every opportunity to tell her how she'd ruined her life—and that there were *places* she could go to get her health back.

Lacey coughed, deep and hoarse. Okay, so her health was failing—she would give them that. But she could have figured out the whole parenting thing if her baby had lived. Right now maybe they'd be walking hand in hand, going to the toy store.

She stood in front of a shop at the mall and saw a woman walk out, holding hands with a little boy who clutched a fuzzy orange ball in his other hand.

"Just like that," she mumbled. Teenage girls nearby looked at her and laughed. She glared in return and followed the mother and her son.

Lacey had always imagined that she had been pregnant with a daughter but now realized it must have been a boy, and he was *right there*!

She hurried faster. They were leaving the mall.

A child at Christmas. Yes, that's it. She wanted a child for Christmas, and no one was going to stop her from having one.

Outside, the woman picked up the boy and turned the corner. His head bobbed around but his stocking hat stayed on. The mother walked briskly to the nearby coffee shop, opened the heavy door, and placed the toddler on the floor inside.

Lacey followed.

She didn't look at the chalkboard menu on the wall. Didn't make eye contact with the woman behind the register or the old man sitting at a table. She just stared at the boy.

I'm going to have a son! Yippee! She was so happy and excited that she could hardly stay quiet. But she knew she must. As soon as she saw the mother look away and start talking to the person filling up a paper cup with coffee, Lacey scooped the child and darted out the door.

Nobody paid her a bit of attention. She blended in with all of the other women and their children walking in and out of the mall to go Christmas shopping. Lacey rushed to her car in the parking lot and put the toddler in the backseat.

"Mama?" The boy's lip quivered as he stared at her.

"Yes, little one. Let's put on your seatbelt. I could get into trouble if I don't have you strapped in!"

After she secured the clip, she scooted into the driver's seat and turned on the ignition.

"Merry Christmas to me!" she gushed.

—⚯—

"What's your address again?" Lacey asked her sister on a pay phone outside a convenience store in Omaha.

"You're really coming?" Lydia's voice sounded enthusiastic.

"Yes, my son and I would like to join you for Christmas, if it's okay."

"Oh, Lace, I've thought about you every day for the past two and a half years and wondered how you two were doing. I can't wait to meet him."

"Okay, we'll be arriving tonight."

Lacey looked at the child sitting in her car. They had already been driving for two hours, and he had fallen asleep. His hat was on his lap, revealing his unique hair. Those curls might be a problem. She couldn't have anyone think that he was that other woman's son.

She bit her lip. She didn't want to leave him in the car but couldn't take him inside the store and risk someone taking him from her. She covered up the sleeping boy with a warm comforter that she kept in her trunk and then ran into the store.

Amidst the blending together of shoppers' voices, Lacey could hear holiday tunes as she hurried through the aisles. She hated places this busy and loud; already she felt claustrophobic.

Must. Get. Out. Of. Here.

She pulled a hanger off a rack, closed her eyes, and gritted her teeth at the sound of a child's shrill cry nearby. She opened her eyes and continued walking briskly.

Why was everyone staring at her? *Stop staring!*

Lacey bit the inside of her cheek and tasted blood. She pushed through a group of people who were standing in front of the candy section.

"Hey!" one of them yelled, giving her an annoyed expression.

She looked into their eyes, challenging, and stuffed a bag against the inside of her elbow before she continued walking.

Almost done. Just one more thing. I can make it.

Lacey coughed, loud and deep, and shoppers around scattered away.

Oh get over it.

People always looked at her like she was going to give them a disease. Her breathing was often wheezy even though she rarely smoked; it was just the way it was. She spit on the floor and smiled smugly at a horrified shopper who passed her.

When she arrived in the check-out line, she carefully counted out the correct amount of change to give to the cashier—glad that she'd gotten some cash this week, as her ways of making money weren't exactly predictable.

The person behind the cash register appeared to be trying not to stare and, once again, Lacey felt that the world was against her.

"Problem?" her voice dripped with sarcasm as she slammed the money on the belt.

The woman counted the money and shook her head. "No problem. Have a good day."

Lacey snatched the plastic sack that contained an electric razor, a boy's 2T outfit, and some M&Ms. She relaxed once she returned to her vehicle. The child in the backseat was still asleep.

"Wake up," she said softly as she sat down next to him. "I got you a treat!"

The boy's eyelids flickered open. His lower lip quivered when he first saw her, but then he relaxed and reached for the sack of M&Ms.

"What's your name, kid?" Lacey asked.

He stared at her, expressionless. Two chubby fingers reached into the bag of M&Ms and pulled out a red piece of candy.

"What's your name?" she asked again.

He chewed the M&M with his mouth open, while a small drool of chocolate dripped down his chin.

"Do you talk?"

The boy nodded.

"Well then, speak. What's your name?"

"Ace" is what Lacey heard as the child grabbed another piece of candy.

"Ace? Okay, Ace. I'm Lacey. I know you probably like that coat you're wearing and those clothes . . . but I'm going to have to throw them away at the next rest stop, and then we're gonna have some real fun and shave your head!"

CHAPTER SIXTEEN

Lydia Feller's heart was thumping. Nothing made her as nervous as seeing her sister. It was such dysfunction—she loved and missed Lacey terribly each time that the woman took off and didn't keep in touch, yet their time together was never pleasant. Lydia always felt defeated when her sister left.

She blamed her father. Lacey never knew that the reason their dad left was because their mother kicked him out after he threw toddler Lacey across the room during one of his drunken rages. Their mother had threatened that if he ever returned, she would put him in jail.

Lydia had been only five, but she'd seen the whole incident from where she peeked through the bedroom door. Lacey wouldn't stay in bed. She kept insisting on another sip of water or a hug from her mom.

Her dad had bellowed, "Get that kid in bed!"

Lydia saw her little sister's body shiver. She was so petite, so small and young-looking for her age.

I must help her.

But Lydia hadn't. She'd been too scared, just didn't have the courage. She stood quiet, staring, as her father picked up the child and tossed her like a ball. Even though as an adult, she knew that there was nothing she could have done at age five, she still carried the guilt.

Lacey had hit her head hard—was that to blame for her erratic behavior in the years that followed? Or, was it drugs that Lydia had caught her doing already at twelve years old? Or, a genetic mental illness? There was no doubt she was unstable, and Lydia felt there was more than just bipolar disorder, which Lacey had been diagnosed with years before.

Her sister was unpredictable at best. For Lydia, as the mother of four, she worried most about her children's safety when their aunt was around. As soon as she'd hung up the phone from talking to Lacey, she called her husband to make sure he'd be home around 9:30 when she expected them to arrive. It was the busiest season at Feller's Apple Orchard/Pumpkin Patch/Tree Farm—a family business started by her husband's parents, who were farmers. After they died, Daniel became owner. They were open year-round but were most popular in the fall and winter, when families from all over the state came for caramel apples, kettle corn, hayrides, duck races, pony rides, a corn pit and maze . . . and to pick out the perfect Christmas tree.

"Your sister is coming over *tonight*?"

"Yes, Daniel, and please treat her with respect."

There was a pause. "Of course."

"Thank you. I really appreciate it. You do remember that she has a child now. A little boy."

"Oh." His voice lost its edge. "That's right. I pray he's in decent shape."

Daniel was the youngest of three children in his family; his sisters were several years older and lived out of state. When they first started dating, he'd told Lydia he wanted ten of their own.

They had met right when she was starting to give up hope of ever finding true love. After she graduated from high school, her mom and Kevin had decided they'd had enough of parenthood. They washed their hands of Lacey's problems and left the United

States. Even though they never would have been candidates for the parents-of-the-year award, Lydia was still shocked at how easily they walked away. They hardly kept in touch with her, and Lydia felt the responsibility of caring for her sister. There was no time between that and waiting tables for her to have any kind of life of her own. Plus, every man she dated turned out to be a dud; she had written off relationships until one day when the most handsome man she'd ever seen walked into the restaurant where she worked.

He was of black Irish descent—thick, dark hair, deep brown eyes, and a five o'clock shadow. She could tell that he was a few years older, and the way that he looked at her wasn't like other men.

The prettier sister was what Lacey always called her. "Men literally drool in your presence."

For a couple of years, Lydia had gotten carried away with giving in to the attention that males gave her until she realized Lacey was trying to compete.

I need to be a better example to her. I'm more than just my looks.

Lydia wanted a man who respected and valued her—and Daniel was just that. After several times of coming into her restaurant, he asked her out. Dinner and a movie. He put his arm around her at the theater (laughing later that his arm became sore but he didn't want to move it), and then that Sunday to church. She'd never been—ever in her life—but finally felt she was where she belonged. It was home. She gave herself to the Lord not long after that. Her first twenty years had been rough, but the ten since then had been everything she had ever wanted and hoped for herself; not a day went by that she didn't give praise to the Lord and appreciate how Daniel had always accepted and adored her, flaws and all.

At 9:30 on the dot, a station wagon from the early 1980s parked in the driveway. Lydia looked out her living room window and pulled at her sweater that was sticking to her. Despite it being cold, she was sweating.

Lydia had turned on the lights outside and could see that the back of the car was filled with clothes and a pillow and even a sack of bread. Her stomach became heavy. The vehicle was her sister's home.

She was glad that her kids were all in bed upstairs and unable to witness whatever kind of shape Lacey was in. But the downside was that Lydia was on her own. Daniel had just called minutes before to say that he was leaving the tree farm now.

Lydia sucked in her breath as Lacey picked up a small child from the backseat. Where was his coat? He was dressed in a t-shirt and sweat pants. And the carseat? *Oh Lacey!* Lydia knew instantly that her sister hadn't changed. If she didn't even have warm clothes or a carseat for her toddler, what other dangerous things was she doing?

Lydia walked to her front door and opened it just as they approached the step.

"Sis," Lacey said with a calm grin as if they talked every day rather than every three years.

"Hello." Lydia took a deep breath and tried to relax her pounding heart. "Please, come in."

"Nice house." Lacey's sarcasm wasn't lost on her sister.

Daniel's family business had been successful. The Fellers lived in a red brick, five bedroom, four bathroom home near Colorado Springs. Lydia considered herself upper-middle class, but to her sister she knew that they appeared very well off.

"Who do we have here?" Lydia bent down to smile at the boy.

"This is my son, Ace." Lacey smiled proudly. "I'm just like you now. I'm a mom. Suzy Homemaker. Have any fruitcake?"

Lydia felt her eyes widen, but Lacey didn't notice; she was already walking to the kitchen. She ran her fingertip across the smooth granite counter top. Her nails were dirty, like her clothes, and her hair was pulled back into a ponytail. At first Lydia thought Lacey's hair was wet, but then she realized it just hadn't been washed recently. Lacey's teeth were yellowish brown, her chin was broken out with pimples, and she had a disturbing cough. Lydia was surprised that the toddler looked clean—that was good, at least.

"Hi, little guy!"

Lacey hardly looked up at the sight of Lydia and Ace meeting; she seemed more jittery by the second.

"Uh, I don't have any fruitcake, but I can make you a sandwich and get you a drink or something."

Before Lacey answered, Tori, the youngest child, began crying from upstairs.

"Do you like babies, Ace? Mine just woke up. I'll go get her, and you can meet her!"

"How many do you have now?" Lacey studied the pictures and artwork on the refrigerator.

"Four," Lydia called over her shoulder as she hurried upstairs.

"Is someone here?" Jason, the oldest, came out of his bedroom.

"Yes. Your Aunt Lacey. Why don't you go down and say hi?"

He appeared to regret waking up. At eight years old, Jason knew the story of his absent family member, but his siblings did not.

Lydia pushed open Tori's door. The nine-month-old girl had pulled herself up to a standing position and was red-faced, straining to get out.

"Hey, sweet girl."

Fraternal twins Monica and Miranda were five and as girly and delicate as Jason was rough and tumble. They had also come out of their rooms in matching Minnie Mouse nightgowns.

"Come on girls, let's go downstairs and meet your cousin. His name is Ace," Lydia urged as she bounced Tori around, which quieted her sobs.

They all walked downstairs and saw that Ace was throwing an orange ball around.

"Fun ball." Lydia picked up the bright, fuzz-covered ball with her free hand and studied it before handing it back to the boy. "I've never seen anything like this."

The toddler looked bashful at the other children until the oldest smiled.

"Hi, I'm Jason. These are my sisters, Monica and Miranda and Tori."

Ace squirmed like a crab trying to fit back into its shell.

"Hey, Lace, the last time you saw Jason, he was in diapers. And you haven't met the girls." Lydia peeked into the kitchen, but her sister wasn't there.

"Where'd your mom go?" she asked the boy.

"Mama?" He looked around, hopeful.

With what felt like a rock in her stomach, Lydia put Tori down and ran to the front door, ready to open it, just as Lacey walked in with a backpack.

"What are you looking so freaked out about?"

"I . . . I thought you'd left."

"Geeze. I just got here. But, actually, I do have a headache. I got a new job. It really uses my brain, ya know? Have to be real smart to do it. Is there somewhere I can lay down?"

"Oh . . . yes, we have a guest bedroom. Um, let me show you where you can stay."

Lydia whispered to Jason, "Can you watch Ace and the girls for a minute, please?"

The boy nodded.

Lydia led her sister downstairs to the finished basement. Did she really have a job? She'd have to ask Lacey more about it tomorrow. She prayed it was respectable. She was uncomfortable with the way that her sister was so jumpy as she studied the home theater and wet bar . . . what if Lacey planned to call her friends tonight to rob the place? Lydia knew that she couldn't trust the woman, but she also couldn't bear *not* to let her into the house. Lacey would always be the little girl whose body she saw land hard on the floor. Lydia remembered how, after their mom threw their dad out that night, they piled into a car, not much different from the station wagon Lacey now drove, and went to the hospital with a completely made-up story.

Lacey was okay, aside from getting the wind knocked out of her and some bruising. Their mom had taken them out for ice cream after leaving the ER. They'd all slept together that night, the three of them in their mother's bed, and Lydia held her sister close, promising to always be there for her. She could still feel the silk of Lacey's hair underneath her hands as she stroked her head, could smell the leftover scents on her from the hospital, and could hear her breaths become shallow as she drifted off to sleep in her arms.

"Here you go. There's a bathroom right there, towels in this closet—please let me know if there's anything else I can get you."

"Thank you," Lacey said sincerely, grabbing her older sister's arm.

Lydia, still tense, nodded. "Sure."

"You know I love you, right?"

"Yes."

The two women hugged. The sound of the garage door let Lydia know that her husband was home.

"That's Daniel; do you want to come up and say hello?"

Lacey's gravelly cough echoed from deep inside her lungs. She pulled away, tapping her leg with her hand at the same time that her foot jerked. "Nah. I haven't slept well lately. I'm going to lay down and, if you don't mind, just stay here till morning."

"What about Ace?"

"Oh. Right. Yeah . . . you can do whatever it is you do with a two-year-old."

Lydia couldn't hide her bewilderment. She was sure her face resembled a distorted fun house mirror.

"Oh—okay . . . I guess I'll see you in the morning, then."

"Goodnight, sleep tight, and don't let the bed bugs bite!" Lacey repeated the phrase their mother used to always say before bed.

If only bed bugs were still the worst of their fears.

CHAPTER SEVENTEEN

Ace was a cute kid, both in appearance and personality. He seemed so . . . secure. Lydia was surprised. She didn't expect Lacey to have a child that looked and acted so healthy. Maybe she'd been wrong. Maybe her sister really was a good mother.

They put an air mattress on Jason's floor for the little boy to sleep on that night. Lydia had forgotten to ask her sister if Ace had a special stuffed animal or blanket, but it seemed he was perfectly content holding the orange ball. *What a funny comfort item,* she thought, chuckling.

"How did Lacey seem?" Daniel asked, turning off the fireplace in the sitting area of their bedroom. He'd been reading while his wife prepared for bed. The 10 pm newscast was also on their bedroom TV; Lydia heard the words "missing child" and "Iowa" as she came out of the master bathroom.

"I couldn't really tell. It was such a short amount of time that I talked to her before she went downstairs, and she seemed so hyper and distracted. I hope that we can chat more tomorrow. I think Ace is a good sign, though. He seems like a wonderful little boy."

"For sure. He makes our kids look like monsters."

Lydia laughed as she shut off the television and climbed into bed. It was true. Jason had been colicky as an infant, the twins had gone above and beyond the terrible two's with temper tantrums and attitudes, and Tori refused to eat any solid food yet.

"It's just weird that she didn't want to hug or say goodnight to him. It almost seemed like she forgot he was even here!"

"Well, even an improved Lacey is still Lacey." Daniel lay down next to his wife.

"I know you don't think much of her, but she's my only sister."

"No, I get it. I want you to have a good relationship with her. I just want you to prepare yourself that she might take off in the night. Fortunately, we have a security system and would at least be notified."

Lydia sighed. "I hope not. I really hope she sticks around this time."

———m———

The next morning, Lydia awoke to a toddler boy's scream. She had to blink a few times before the previous day's events registered in her mind and she realized that it was her nephew.

Stumbling out of bed, she hurried down the hallway to Jason's room. She knelt down and wrapped her arms around Ace, whose cheeks were wet with tears. Jason squinted at her and then rolled over.

"Mama?" The toddler's nose was running, and he hiccupped.

"I'll go get her, sweetheart. Let me take you in to your Uncle Daniel."

Lydia lifted the boy off the floor and brought him into her room, where she set him down on the bed. She was glad to see that he'd calmed down. He was still clutching the soft ball.

Lydia nudged her husband. "I'm going to wake up my sister. Do you want to get Ace some breakfast?"

"Yeah, sure." Daniel yawned and looked at the clock. It was only about a half hour before he usually got up for work.

Lydia smiled and waved to her nephew. "I'll be right back, okay?" Ace nodded.

She made her way to the basement and turned on the light. It was colder downstairs than she'd realized last night, but maybe Lacey didn't notice it as much since she'd spent the past ten years living homeless half the time.

One of the girls had left a doll lying in the middle of the beige carpet. She picked it up and then knocked on the guest bedroom door.

"Lace? It's me. Ace is awake and asking for you."

There was no answer, so Lydia knocked again.

"Sis. Can I open the door?" She put her hand on the knob and slowly turned it, expecting to hear Lacey shout something about privacy and slam the door as she had when she was fourteen. But there was just silence.

"Lacey?" She peeked into the bedroom and saw her sister sprawled on the bed. She was still in her clothes from the day before, but her hair was no longer in a ponytail. Her skin was completely white. On the small night stand next to the bed was a needle.

"Lacey!" Lydia shrieked, running over to the sister she'd always wanted so much to protect.

But it was too late. She was cold. Lifeless. Lydia didn't know much about death, but she knew enough to know that her sister had been deceased for quite a while.

She screamed her husband's name as loud as she could, holding the petite woman in her arms, similar to the way she had twenty-five years before.

"No! No! No! No!"

"What is it? Lydia?" He called as he raced down the stairs. He stopped in the doorway as soon as he saw Lacey in his wife's arms.

"She's gone, Daniel! She's gone!"

After the ambulance came and paramedics confirmed Lacey's death, the Fellers were asked which funeral home they wanted to use. Lydia struggled to keep it together. It had finally happened—what she'd feared for decades. Her sister had died of an accidental overdose at the age of twenty-seven, after injecting herself with methamphetamine. Of course, an autopsy would be done, but Lydia knew that it was a long time coming. Of course, it didn't make the loss any less devastating.

At least, in a strange way, she had been able to say goodbye. And, Lacey hadn't died on the streets, leaving Ace unprotected.

Poor Ace.

When Daniel ran upstairs to call 9-1-1, he'd instructed Jason to keep his cousin and siblings away from the basement. They could hear the children taking turns with frustrated cries, but it would be too traumatizing for Ace to see his mom's condition.

After Lacey's body was carried out of the home, Lydia leaned into her husband and sobbed quietly into his chest.

"What's going to happen to Ace? When I spoke with my sister three years ago, she told me that the father had left as soon as she found out she was pregnant. I don't know his name and certainly have no idea where he even is."

"The policeman who was here said they'll notify DHS."

"Daniel . . . we can't have him go into the foster care system."

Lydia's husband put his arm around her shoulders and kissed the top of her head. "I agree. I wouldn't expect otherwise. Ace will stay with us."

CHAPTER EIGHTEEN

Thursday, December 21, 1995

The Fellers celebrated Ace's adoption at Chuck E. Cheese. It'd taken a year for the process to be completed. Immediately following Lacey's death, they'd hired a lawyer.

"This is a tricky situation. With your sister being homeless for most of her adult life, it appears that there was never a birth certificate for Ace, or at least we are unable to locate one. And, you don't know where or who she was living with?"

Lydia sighed. "Correct . . . from what I know about her pattern, she'd stay in a state for maybe six months and then move. She always cut ties with everyone . . . never trusted people so she never stayed in touch with anyone . . . no committed boyfriends, although she was with Ace's father off and on for two years. We grew up in Kansas City ourselves, but when I spoke with her two and a half years ago, she was in Tennessee."

"Tennessee? Okay, since that's the last place she was known to be, we'll check their database to make sure that no one who might have more information on Ace's history is looking for them, and we'll serve the unknown father in the newspaper there."

No missing person's reports had been filed in the state of Tennessee for anyone matching Lacey or Ace's description. Custody of their nephew was first obtained through a petition for custody in juvenile court. They filed a petition to terminate parental rights, based on abandonment for willful failure to provide support and visit, at the same time as a petition for adoption in circuit court. An ad was placed, but after thirty days with no word from a possible father, their attorney moved the court for a default judgment and asked to proceed with the termination and adoption. The court granted the attorney's default judgment, terminated the rights of the father, and granted the adoption. A birth certificate was ordered from the state, Ace was given a Social Security number, and he was now their son.

"Thank you so much for helping us to make the process go smoothly." Lydia shook their lawyer's hand at their last court hearing.

"It really helps when there is no one contesting an adoption. Everyone has agreed from the beginning that your nephew should live with you. He's lucky to have you in his life." The lawyer patted the little boy's shoulder. Ace had been required to come to the adoption but otherwise had been able to avoid most of the proceedings and stay sheltered.

By the time of their celebration at Chuck E. Cheese, Lydia was exhausted. Between grieving the death of her sister, adopting Ace, and keeping up with her other children and responsibilities, it had been a busy and hectic year. Lydia felt as if she had lived in her own little bubble. She didn't watch TV and had no clue what was going on in the world. She'd heard that football star O.J. Simpson was found not guilty of murdering his ex-wife, but otherwise didn't stay up-to-date on the news anymore.

Since they didn't know his actual birthday, the boy was given the date that he first came into the Fellers' home—so, it was a double party. After eating pizza and playing games, the family shared a white birthday cake with chocolate frosting and the number three on top.

"Mickey Mouse!" Ace clapped at the wrapping paper when his first present was placed in front of him.

Lydia was relieved that Ace had remained a happy child. Before the funeral, she and Daniel had carefully explained to him that his mother had gone to heaven and now he'd be living with them. The Fellers knew that he probably didn't fully understand, and for months he woke up crying for his mother every single night. Sometimes he still did, but he had latched on to their family and had seemed to adjust.

They had kept his hair in the buzz cut that Lacey gave him, but he hardly resembled the child he'd been a year ago. Now, he was taller and slimmed down, so Ace looked more like a little boy than a toddler. He spoke regularly and was developing interests, such as soccer. She would have to sign him up for his first year in the spring. Lydia felt bad for having kept him inside the past year, as he probably would have loved to visit places like Chuck E. Cheese sooner. Now that the adoption was behind them, though, she planned to do more fun activities with all of her children. She was worn out but happy. Despite the tragic circumstances of losing his mother, Ace had been a wonderful addition to their family. She prayed and thanked her sister daily for the gift of her son. Life was complete.

—✺—

"It's slumber party time!" The eldest Feller children exclaimed after they'd arrived back to the house following Chuck E. Cheese.

Usually, it was tradition for the family to have a slumber party on Thanksgiving night after they hung stockings on the fireplace mantel. Daniel and Lydia always bought everyone matching Christmas pajamas, popped popcorn, and spread out sleeping bags in the middle of the floor. Then, they watched their first Christmas movie of the season. This year, however, they'd been so run down from the chaotic year, that they'd gotten sick with a winter virus and decided to postpone their family slumber party until Ace's big day.

Daniel put this year's video into the VCR and pushed play.

After the opening credits, a woman with long, dark brown hair appeared on screen.

"Mama!" Ace pointed and smiled.

He referred to Lydia as Mom, not because she had ever suggested that he do so, but simply because the other children did, and he copied almost everything they said. She remembered from that first horrific morning at their house when Ace had called for Lacey, that "mama" was his label for her sister.

But the woman on the screen looked nothing like Lydia's sister. She exchanged puzzled looks with Daniel. His forehead creased with concern.

Months before, they discussed that Lacey must have had help raising Ace. There was no other explanation for how good a shape he was in. When the Fellers took him to the pediatrician for the first time, their doctor had been impressed.

"There is absolutely no sign of abuse or neglect. He appears healthier than most of my patients who live in the most attentive of families. He doesn't seem to have suffered from ear infections, and his teeth are in great shape—as if they've been brushed regularly for over a year. It is not my belief that this child was homeless. I think your sister must have had a proper home for him."

"Then why hasn't anyone reported her missing?"

It was the same question they'd had once they discovered there were no items in Lacey's vehicle for Ace—no clothes, no toys, not even diapers. Luckily, they'd had a few in his size leftover from the twins. They must have been living somewhere after all—but where? They'd been unable to track down any employment records, so Lydia had a feeling her sister had been lying about the new job. It seemed more likely that her money was made illegally.

Everything regarding Lacey's life the past three years was a mystery to the Fellers. The only guests at her funeral were Daniel, Lydia, their four children, Ace, and Lacey's mom and stepdad—who still lived out of the country and stayed only two days before returning home as quickly as they could. They hardly showed any emotion during the service, and their eyes were transparent when meeting Ace and their other grandchildren. Lydia was surprised they came at all and not disappointed that they stayed only forty-eight hours.

Now, she wondered if there had been a dark-haired woman who helped Lacey care for her son. Lydia had never trusted her sister's judgment, had never seen her think about consequences or put someone's needs above her own . . . but maybe having a baby had triggered something within her. Maybe she had been smart enough to not be selfish for once and instead let someone more stable assist her in raising Ace.

If there was someone wise in Lacey's life, wouldn't they have known that she had a sister and tried to contact the Fellers? Or, even if they hadn't known about her family—wouldn't they have been worried about the welfare of Ace when Lacey took off with him? Wouldn't they have filed a police report? Something didn't make sense, but Lydia couldn't pinpoint *what* exactly.

Ace couldn't help—by the time he'd started talking, he didn't seem to remember anything from his former life. When she and Daniel asked him questions, his answer changed depending on who and when he was asked. Even *how* he was asked played a role—as Lydia noticed that whenever she gave him two options, he most often just repeated the last word she said. It was typical for a toddler but frustrating nonetheless.

Lydia pulled Ace to her and hugged him on her lap, rubbing the spot on his palm where his unique birthmark was. Even though she hadn't given birth to him, she loved him the same as her other children. It had taken a few months—for when he spent the first several weeks screaming in the night, Lydia hadn't known what to do. She'd never functioned well on no sleep and was exhausted from taking care of five children every day. The ideas that she'd used to get the others to sleep didn't work on Ace. In those middle-of-the-night hours, she'd often cursed her sister for choosing drugs over her child. Lacey had known her family would help her with rehab but had been too stubborn and lost her life because of it. Why was it always Lydia who picked up her family's responsibility? She suffered from stress the same as anyone, and taking care of five children when she was only thirty years old was, at times, overwhelming. Had she made the right decision by adopting Ace, or was she in over her head?

"Please, Lord, let me do right by Ace. I want to raise him to be the man that you want him to be. I want to give him the best life he can have."

One night, Lydia turned on a lullaby CD, and the song "Twinkle Twinkle Little Star" played. Ace immediately relaxed.

"Do you like this song, buddy?" she asked as she rubbed his head.

After that, she turned the soft music on whenever he woke up, and he immediately fell back asleep. Pretty soon he stopped waking up at all. With Lydia well-rested, she gained more confidence in her ability to be a mother of five, and she could focus on him more, which allowed her love to grow greater each day. He was a very special soul.

Was there a woman, somewhere out there, who had been first to soothe Ace with "Twinkle, Twinkle Little Star"? If so, where was she? *Who* was she?

CHAPTER NINETEEN

Monday, December 21, 2009

"Happy birthday!" Lydia grinned when Ace came downstairs for breakfast.

She couldn't believe fifteen years had passed since the first day that she'd met him. Ace was a junior in high school now. He was tall and handsome, and his friends teased him that he looked like a blond Jonas brother with his curly hair and lop-sided grin. His eyes were still the brightest of blues, and teenage girls often blushed when meeting his gaze.

But he had eyes only for Rachel. They'd grown up together, had been in the same elementary school homeroom several times, and were in church youth group together in junior high and high school.

Lydia knew that Ace wanted to propose to Rachel as soon as they graduated from high school. She worried about them being too young, but she adored Rachel, and Ace had been such a responsible boy that she was confident he would take on the role of a husband well. Her other children, however, would have given her extreme anxiety had they expressed the same feelings.

Jason was twenty-three and going to medical school in Chicago. He wanted to be an orthopedic surgeon. Living nearly seventeen hours away, Lydia felt out of the loop when it came to his personal life, but he had always been outgoing, driven, and a perfectionist, so she knew that his passion was work right now rather than a relationship.

The twins, Monica and Miranda, were twenty and free spirits. Monica was a writer and majoring in English at The University of California-Berkley, while Miranda was getting her degree in Fashion Design at Kent State. Next semester she would be studying abroad in Paris.

Meanwhile, Tori was fifteen and a sophomore in high school. She was fascinated by religion and couldn't wait to become a minister.

Ace had always been studious and a favorite of the teachers, so Lydia had expected him to go to college—but he was insistent that he wanted to continue to help Daniel with the family business, where he already worked after school.

All of the Fellers had taken on different roles at the apple orchard/pumpkin patch/tree farm throughout the years, but none seemed as interested as Ace in making it their profession.

The children had gone through individual stages where they'd been jealous of the boy who had come into their family unexpectedly, but those phases had been short, and they'd been grateful to have him as part of their life. Likewise, he'd done well with siblings. By age four, he came out of his shell and nearly bounced off the walls with energy that year. He had his difficult moments like the rest of them—he spent nearly his entire kindergarten year whining, had gone through a fibbing phase, and until he was seven or eight, refused to wear any shirt that had buttons, snaps, or zippers and became hysterical if they tried to force him. But, he'd always been a natural rule-follower and a lover of people—and carried himself in a way that people respected rather than took advantage of.

Ace gave Lydia a warm hug. She had made him pancakes, eggs, and sausage, and ushered him to the table where she set his plate. "Thanks, Mom."

She loved making breakfast for her children each morning and couldn't believe that she and Daniel would be empty nesters in a couple of years. All she'd ever wanted was to be a mom. Back when her parents fought or when her mother was preoccupied with Kevin, Lydia used to fantasize about the children that she would have and how happy they would be. She couldn't remember ever going to bed feeling safe and peaceful. She had imagined what it'd be like to stand outside of her house at night and look in to see her parents, embraced by the warm light, tucking her and Lacey in and kissing her cheeks. She wanted that for her children—wanted them to go to bed knowing that they were loved.

It was an incredible reward to know that she had accomplished her purpose in life. Her five children had grown up in the stable home that she'd never had, and they were happy people with Christ at the center of their lives. It was what she focused on whenever she became sad about the last of her children leaving home soon.

It would be nice, however, to travel with Daniel. They'd had a strong marriage all of these years, but due to the chaos of having five children, they hadn't taken many vacations. She was excited about the trips she and her husband were already planning. They would have plenty to do.

"What are you going to do on your first day of winter break?" Lydia asked, scooping food onto a plate for herself.

"I'm planning to help Dad at the tree farm."

"I should have known. Of course you are." Lydia smiled and sat down across from him.

"Where's Tori?"

"Still sleeping. I'll be surprised if she gets out of her pajamas all day."

Ace laughed and then cleared his throat. His face grew serious. "What do you think about me giving Rachel a promise ring for Christmas?"

Lydia cast her gaze downward and took a drink of her orange juice before answering. His question didn't necessarily come as a shock, but she'd hoped to put it off as long as possible.

"I can't really say much, as I was pretty young when I got married. I couldn't wait to get out of my home and start a life of my own, prove to myself that I could do things differently than my parents did and have a good life. But you're even younger than I was. You really have to grow up once you make that commitment. Your dad and I can't help you with finances . . . can you support Rachel? What does she plan to do after high school? Have children? Go to college? Get a job somewhere?"

"Well, actually, I was hoping to talk to Dad about it today when I get to the tree farm. You know how Rachel has worked there a few summers . . . well, once she's family, maybe she can be a part of our family business."

"I see." It wasn't a ridiculous request. She could easily visualize Ace and Rachel having a wedding in two years, staying in their small town, and being co-owners of Feller's together. It was actually a pleasant thought.

"There's still a couple of years before you need to make the decision, so let's spend that time praying that God will make clear what His plan is for you and Rachel. You've been a good kid. You've always stayed out of trouble, and I trust your judgments. If Dad gives you his blessing, then I'll give you mine."

"Thanks, Mom. I really appreciate that."

He had really turned out well, despite her sister having been so unstable. Lydia had never let go of the restless feeling inside of her regarding the years that Ace had spent prior to living with them. She had always been certain that her sister had not raised Ace alone.

She'd decided to join the social networking site, Facebook, that year. Maybe someone would look her up and send a message that would answer her questions about where Ace had lived before Colorado and what his life had been like.

He was clearly a spitting image of his father, for he didn't look anything like Lacey. Nor did he have the red locks that had been dominant in their family—that Lydia and all three of her girls had inherited (Jason shared his father's dark hair).

She had spent hours on several different occasions looking up any possible information about her sister. Internet searches left her frustrated, but Daniel always reminded her that it didn't bother Ace, so it shouldn't bother Lydia.

It was true—they'd never kept Ace's adoption a secret. He had known from the beginning the story of how his mommy had gone to heaven and his aunt and uncle had become his parents. He tried to remember life before coming to the Fellers, but he couldn't. His earliest memory was of his third birthday party and adoption celebration at Chuck E. Cheese. They'd shown him pictures of Lacey, hoping to spark a memory, but he always shook his head and said maybe it was for the best they didn't try to stir up the past if his life hadn't been so good before. He was content, but Lydia didn't know if she would ever be. It was an itch she couldn't scratch.

Now and then, after everyone was in bed, she still filled the Internet search engine with every word she could think of that might unlock the mystery of Lacey's past. Despite a world of blogs and tweets, it was like trying to find a needle in a haystack. She posted questions on message boards and even offered a small reward for anyone who knew information about her sister during her final two years.

As she watched Ace finish his food, it occurred to her that she didn't even know his real birthday. Prior to the day Lacey had arrived on her doorstep with Ace, Lydia had last spoken with her sister in April 1992 and she'd been at least a couple of months pregnant at the time. So maybe his birthday was really November? However, he didn't seem quite two when she had met him. So January then? But that meant Lacey would have called her the minute she found out she was pregnant, and that seemed unlikely. There were so many things that didn't make sense. A few months ago, when kidnapping victim Jaycee Dugard was found, it had even crossed her mind that maybe Ace wasn't Lacey's son at all—which was absurd, right? Lydia was so desperate to find out the truth that she was grasping at straws.

Please, God, give me the answers, she prayed. *I know that there's more to this story—I can feel it.*

Feller's Apple Orchard/Pumpkin Patch/Tree Farm was busy for being just four days before Christmas. It had been an extra snowy winter, which often made families wait until the last minute to shop for a real Christmas tree. Today it was approximately forty degrees—a scorcher for this time of year—so Ace was not surprised to see so many families out. Or maybe it was because of their indoor activity—today was Santa's last day, having spent the past three weeks reading books to children and smiling for pictures as parents put cameras in front of their little ones sitting on his lap. Because Feller's was well-known for being a Christian business, the books that their Santa read were always based on the story of Jesus. Children were all given candy canes with crosses taped to the front and the words *Merry CHRISTmas*!

Ace held the door of their renovated barn open for a family heading inside. He smiled at the three children who were bouncing up and down.

"There he is! There he is!" They pointed to the white-bearded man in the red suit.

Ace followed them inside and surveyed the area for his dad. He could see through the open window of Daniel's office that he wasn't sitting at his desk.

"Must be outside," he murmured, urgently grabbing a pair of gloves from his pocket to search the tree farm. The ball that he always carried with him in his coat, a habit since it became his comfort item when he was two years old, fell to the ground and rolled to the edge of the furnace.

As he bent over to pick up the ball, he smelled the distinct odor of gas. He stood up and stared at the furnace. His dad had mentioned that it had gone out days ago but claimed it had been fixed. Ace rolled the ball back and forth in his hands and looked around the room. A little girl dressed in a gold tutu and sweater spun around in circles, laughing. A family near the bakery section was sharing samples of desserts and smiling at each other. A mother sat off to the side, nursing an infant under a wrap.

Ace knew he needed to get his father, but this seemed serious. Dangerous. He didn't know much about furnaces but knew this wasn't good. He couldn't walk out of the building and leave all of these people with a gas leak. They should get out immediately. Or was he overreacting?

The kids he had walked in with were excitedly climbing onto Santa's lap. They all had one lone dimple in their cheeks—they could have been on a commercial or a magazine ad, they were so cute. He shoved the ball back into his pocket and decided that it was worth the risk of looking like an idiot.

"Hey!" he shouted. "I'm Ace Feller, and this is my family's business. Not to alarm anyone, but it appears there's a problem with our furnace. I know this is an inconvenience, but can I please have everyone evacuate? I think we need to get a professional in here."

Voices that had been trampling over each other quieted down. Heads turned to face him, and those standing in the lines looked a bit annoyed, but the Santa Claus appeared alarmed beneath his beard.

The man in the red and white suit leapt to his feet. "You heard the kid; let's all move out!"

Customers who hadn't heard Ace were scrambling around, shouting, "What? What's going on?"

The word spread as everyone in the building filtered outside. Ace darted through the rows of trees until he spotted his father.

"Dad! Dad! There's a—"

Before Ace could finish his sentence, there was a loud noise and then a fireball as the building nearby collapsed into flames.

"No!" Daniel slapped each of his hands to the sides of his head and took off running toward the explosion.

"Wait! Everybody's out!" Ace yelled, grabbing his father's sleeve.

"What?" Daniel's face was ashen, and his cheeks were sunk in.

"There was a gas leak in the furnace; I was just coming to tell you."

People around were screaming, children were crying, and there was dirt and debris everywhere.

"Oh, thank God," Ace's father ran his hands through his hair and then shouted to the crowd. "Is anyone hurt? Is everyone okay?"

Men and women were hugging, parents were scooping up their children to hold them tight, and others brushed dust from their clothing—but although there were some cuts and scrapes, nobody seemed to be seriously injured.

"Is there anyone not accounted for?" Daniel yelled.

The customers at Feller's all looked around at each other in disbelief, now sharing a bond of thanks forever.

"I can't believe this. Amazing." Ace's dad grabbed him by the neck and pulled him close. Sirens blared in the distance. The fire was soon put out. It was a true miracle—not only no fatalities, but no one was critically injured.

With tears in his eyes, Daniel put an arm around Ace again. "Do you realize what you did today? You saved at least one hundred lives. If you hadn't gotten them out when you did . . . wow." He shook his head. "Look at you—so calm. I've never known anyone to handle stress as good as you. You did well, Ace. I'm so proud to be your dad."

CHAPTER TWENTY

Christmas 2013

Lydia couldn't sleep. In 2011, there'd been a response to one of her posts on a message board. Reid Gibson, a man of African-American decent, had claimed to be the father of Lacey's child.

Hey, I knew Lacey. Me and her went out Halloween 1990–March 1992. Sorry, I was messed up and freaked when she told me she was pregnant and I ran. Heard she lost the baby, tho, so don't know nothing about an Ace. Didn't know she died til I saw this post.

How was that possible? Her sister had lost a baby and became pregnant by another man's child in the same year?

"I hate to be the one to break it to you, but it happens." Daniel massaged her tense shoulders.

"But that doesn't fit. I talked to Lacey in April 1992, and then she showed up here December 1994. Ace can't be her second pregnancy—or else he'd be younger than he is." She thought about his blond hair and blue eyes. He clearly was not the spitting image of Reid. "Do you think she thought Reid was the father, but after the baby was born, she knew he wasn't? And so she lied to him about having a miscarriage?"

"Hon, Lacey's life was about as complicated as they come. There's no point in stressing yourself out with this. We'll never know the extent of it."

But this past May, when the three girls in Cleveland were found after being held in a house against their will for a decade, she'd decided to search national missing kids websites for all children in the USA who disappeared twenty years ago. She felt guilty for thinking that her sister could be a child abductor, so she didn't act immediately on the idea. After waiting seven months, she couldn't take the anxiety anymore. Today had been the twentieth Christmas that she'd spent with Ace and she was still restless about his background. So, once each of her children had gone back to their own homes, she clicked on every photograph from the "15–20 years ago" category until she was exhausted.

Her laptop was on the arm of the couch where she sat, sipping her hot green tea, when she saw his face.

The tea burned her tongue.

She shut her laptop.

No. No. It can't be.

Daniel was watching TV in their finished basement—also known as his man cave. But she couldn't move to go get him. She couldn't swallow. A lump in her throat grew bigger. She stared at the cross hanging on her living room wall.

Lydia had been right! He was on the list! Someone had been searching for him after all! His name wasn't Ace . . . but Chase. How long had this website been online? Had his picture really been there all along? Why hadn't she thought to look sooner?

Her body shook. She placed her mug on the nearby coffee table and pressed her fingertips to her eyelids. Was this really happening? Her unsettled feeling finally being validated?

She opened her laptop back up and looked at the photograph of the little boy that she remembered so well. She hadn't seen his curly hair until he was about three and a half years old, but otherwise the picture on the screen was identical to those she had in her photo albums from Christmas 1994.

What did this mean? That Lacey had *kidnapped* him? Was Lydia supposed to call the police? She had adopted a child that she had no right to!

February. His birthday was really February. *Des Moines, Iowa.* She hadn't even known her sister ever lived there. *A coffee shop.* He was last seen with his mother at a coffee shop?

The poor woman!

Lydia wanted to call her. Ace's parents—*Chase's* parents— might think he was dead! Would she be able to still have hope if one of her children had gone missing nineteen years ago? Her stomach turned, and she began gagging. She slapped her hand over her mouth and ran to the bathroom.

This was worse than she had ever thought. All of these years she only hoped to find someone who had known her sister or Ace. She never would have believed there was an entire family who he'd belonged to. She'd been looking in the wrong places. Hadn't wanted to think the worst about her sister. But Lacey had committed a federal crime. She had ripped a family's heart out. She had *stolen* someone else's son . . . and Lydia helped! For nineteen years she had unknowingly kept a child from the parents that God had given him to. No doubt they had experienced incredible grief, while she had lived all these years carefree and feeling *thankful* to Lacey. What terrible, awful irony! She wasn't one to swear, but she really had to bite her tongue at thoughts of her sister right now.

How could you? How could you?! Her eyes brimmed with tears.

"Daniel!" she called as she flushed the toilet. She washed her hands and was brushing her teeth when her husband came in.

"What's wrong? What happened?" he asked.

Lydia shook her head. In the mirror, she saw that her eyes were bloodshot and her face was swollen. She rinsed her mouth and pressed her palms on the counter, leaning over the sink and still feeling sick.

"Are you okay?"

Lydia shook her head. "I suspected . . . all along I suspected . . . I just didn't listen . . . didn't want to believe it."

"Didn't want to believe what?"

"Ace. It's about Ace."

"What about him?"

"He's not my blood! Lacey did an evil thing. A truly evil thing. Come here." Lydia motioned for her husband to follow her back to the living room.

She showed him the computer screen. The name Chase Tate was written under big, red, bold letters that read MISSING— PLEASE HELP BRING ME HOME. There was even an age-progression photo that looked remarkably like the adult that their adopted son had become. Underneath were the words *Anyone Having Information Should Contact the Iowa Division of Criminal Investigation.* A special agent's name and number were provided.

"He was *kidnapped*?" Daniel stood frozen, staring at the screen. "But how could we not have known this? How could we have adopted him if there was a missing report filed for him?"

Lydia paced the room. "There's better technology now than there was twenty years ago. Now, anyone can find out in an instant if a child in the US has gone missing *today*. Even back then, if we had suspected he wasn't Lacey's, the police would have figured out who he was within minutes . . . but we had no reason to think that he wasn't hers. Because of me. Because of *my* insistence that she was pregnant with a baby two years before, and her history of living on the streets. He was her child, there was no question. At the time, we were all so preoccupied with Lacey's death and the adoption that we didn't hear anything about Chase two states over."

Lydia was glad that Daniel put his arms around her at that point because she thought she was going to either be sick again or faint.

"Should we call that number now? What do we do?" She put her hand to her chest.

"We better tell Ace first. He's an adult now. He should know before we call the authorities. This is going to change all of our lives. We need to each digest this first."

"Yes. Daniel, I'm not feeling well."

"It'll be okay. It's going to be okay."

Lydia lay awake all night.

—⚹—

The next morning, Daniel called Ace. He and Rachel lived a couple of miles away with their two-year-old son, Miles. As planned, they'd gotten married just two months after graduating from high school and worked together at Feller's. Miles might as well have been a clone of Ace. It was creepy, actually, just how much he resembled Ace at the same age. Aside from the yellow tint to the older photographs, no one would be able to tell pictures of the two apart.

Lydia cleaned the kitchen as her husband told Ace that he needed to come over. She was still scrubbing the same spot on her counter when her All-American-looking son walked inside.

He'd never resembled any of them. Ace was so tall, so much taller than the rest of their family. The Feller children had her petite build. She had always assumed that Ace's birth father must have been tall since Lacey was short herself. But it was Alan and Arianna who were tall. The lump in her throat from last night returned.

"Hey, what's up, guys?" Ace said as he pulled a chair out from the table and sat down. He leaned back and clasped his hands behind his neck. Lydia didn't look up. "Mom? Are you all right?"

Daniel put his hand on top of Lydia's. "You're going to dig a hole in the counter."

Lydia threw down her rag and crossed her arms. "How do you suppose we tell him?"

She had thought all night about ways to break the news to Ace, but none seemed good.

"Tell me what? You're sort of making me nervous."

Daniel cleared his throat. "Your mom uncovered some information about your past before you came to live with us."

"Oh wow." Ace sat up straight and rubbed his palms on his knees.

Lydia continued. "That's right. You know how I've always had a feeling there was more to your story? Well, it has turned out to be a far bigger deal than any of us could have imagined. Your name . . . it's really Chase."

Her son laughed. "Okay. Cool. Ace is like my nickname then."

Lydia didn't smile. "Your last name is Tate."

"Oh." Ace's face fell. "You found my dad?"

Lydia looked to Daniel for help. Her husband took a seat across from Ace and stared down at the table. "What your mother found is your picture in the national database for missing children. It appears that Lacey was not your birth mom. She kidnapped you from a couple in Des Moines, Iowa, just hours before she brought you here."

Ace's eyes grew wide. He looked from parent to parent as if he were hoping that one of them would say that they were joking.

Lydia joined the men at the table and gave Ace a hug. "I think that since you're twenty-one . . . or I guess almost twenty-one since your real birthday is February . . . it's in your hands on what you want to do with this information. It's a lot to take in, so please know that we are there for you."

"Wow . . . wow." Ace leaned forward and put his elbows on the table. His fingers wiped at his eyes, and he buried his face in his hands.

"Would you like to see the website?"

He nodded.

Daniel brought the laptop around in front of Ace.

Lydia pointed to the screen. "There you are. Just like I remember, except she must have shaved your head before she brought you here."

"Incredible." Ace said after he was done reading the short paragraph. "Have you tried searching the Internet for me, now that you know my real name?"

Lydia shook her head. "No . . . I was so stunned by this last night."

Ace typed "Chase Tate" into the search engine. The first website to appear was completely devoted to finding him. As he clicked around on the different links, he realized that his birth parents were the website owners.

"Alan and Arianna." He took a deep breath as he stared at a Christmas photo taken several years ago. "I have another sister. CeCe."

Tears burned the back of Lydia's eyes as she stared at the faces of the family who were strangers yet had been the most important people in the Fellers' lives without ever knowing.

Ace glanced at her and then back at the computer. He closed down the website and stood up.

"Wow," he said again. "You're right, this is a lot. But you know what? It doesn't change anything. This is still my life, you're still my parents, and I still love you. I'm not going to leave Ace Feller behind and start calling myself Chase Tate. I know that we're now aware of a crime, but I'm going to have to consult the big man upstairs to figure out what's the best move for me to make—and talk to my wife."

Ace and his parents hugged. Lydia felt the lump finally leave her throat. He had handled the news better than she ever could have. Life was never going to be the same, but for some reason God had chosen now to answer her prayer of questions she'd had for years. That meant it *had* to be okay.

CHAPTER TWENTY-ONE

The woman with dark hair was nice and smelled like lavender. Ace had never told anyone, but he did have one memory prior to living with the Fellers. They were standing in a toy store, and the brunette handed him the soft, orange ball. He couldn't recall what she said to him—but her voice was gentle, and she had a warm laugh. There was no one else he would have rather been with.

The orange ball was no longer vibrant, and the fuzz was all worn off now, but when he didn't carry it in his pocket, it had sat on his nightstand the entire time he was growing up. There was something about that ball . . . pure comfort. Now he knew why. It was given to him by his mother.

As a parent himself now, he knew that the woman must have countless memories of him. She had probably relived each one of them every day for over nineteen years.

He couldn't offer her the same. Would she expect to pick up where they left off? The only family that he knew was the Fellers. It had never bothered him to know that he was adopted while growing up. He had always been thankful that he grew up with Daniel and Lydia rather than on the streets with Lacey. He didn't spend time dwelling on the past or obsessing about what his first two years had been like.

But Alan and Arianna looked like a perfectly fine couple. They didn't deserve to have their son taken away from them. In one moment, Ace's life no longer made sense to him. He might as well have egg on his face—his entire identity was fake. Even though the kidnapping had been out of his control, he felt shame and embarrassment. The last thing he wanted to do right now was to meet the couple in Iowa. Ignorance had been bliss.

Spring 2014

The sun set and rose again day after day, week after week. Via the Internet, Ace learned everything he could about his birth family and life as Chase. People had been looking for him for almost two decades, and he'd had no clue. As much as he disliked that this was the reality of his life, he recognized that nobody ever picked their problems. This situation was his to handle. He met with his pastor regularly, and his wife Rachel most often found him engrossed in his Bible.

> *For I know the plans I have for you, says the Lord. They are plans for good and not for evil, to give you a future and a hope.*
> (Jeremiah 29:11)

> *We can make our plans, but the final outcome is in God's hands.*
> (Proverbs 16:1)

Rachel laid her head on his chest. "You know who you are inside. God gave you a soul before he gave you to any parent. We are not just products of our upbringing. You are my husband, regardless. If anything, you are blessed to find out that there are even more people who love you. This doesn't lessen the family that you were raised in . . . you now have an additional one!"

"I agree." Ace closed his Bible. "I'd like to go see them in person now."

"Really? I'm so happy for you. And them!"

"We've never been to Des Moines. I'll start looking at hotels . . . time to take a family road trip!"

—⁓—

If not for Miles in the backseat, Ace and Rachel might have fallen asleep on the ride from Colorado to Iowa, as it was the most monotonous drive they'd ever taken. Fortunately, Miles kept them busy with requests for snacks and drinks, looking at books, and singing nursery rhymes. They stopped for restrooms and meals along the way, and Miles had passed out for the night by the time they arrived to the Fairfield Inn & Suites in West Des Moines.

"I still think you should call them," Rachel suggested quietly after they'd unpacked their suitcases and crawled into bed. "What if they're on vacation somewhere? Or busy? You can't just show up on their door stop unannounced."

"I know. But it's been almost nineteen and a half years, I can't just tell them over the phone. I want to meet them in person. I saw that Arianna works full-time at a shelter. That's where I've decided we should go tomorrow."

"We? You want Miles and I to come with you?"

Ace touched his wife's chin and tilted her mouth to meet his in a kiss. "I'm glad you came with me on this trip. It wouldn't feel right without you. You and Miles are the most important people in my life, and I want you there when I meet my birth parents."

—⁓—

It was pouring rain when the family awoke the next morning. After they enjoyed a continental breakfast, Ace consulted the maps application on his smartphone. The shelter was located a little over ten miles away from the hotel. They sat in silence on the drive—even Miles must have sensed this was a special day. Ace couldn't remember ever being so nervous in his life. He fiddled with the radio and heat a dozen times. Windshield wipers were on full speed as Ace pulled into the parking lot.

Rachel opened the glove compartment and pulled out a black umbrella.

"You ready?"

Ace held his wife's hand. "Dear Lord, please be with us as we go into this building. Give us the proper words to speak to Arianna Tate. Let our hearts be on the same page. Give us wisdom to know how to move forward. In Jesus' name, amen."

Ace unbuckled Miles from the carseat and rushed to the entrance. The building was newly renovated and looked nicer than he had imagined. The sign inside indicated that there was a food pantry, classroom, expanded housing capacity, clothing closet, and on-site health clinic.

"My nerves have gotten the best of me, I need to make a quick stop at the restroom," Ace whispered to Rachel once they were out of the rain.

Rachel nodded and took Miles from her husband.

"Down!" Miles instructed.

"Shh," Rachel whispered, but obliged her son. Miles took off running.

"Miles Daniel! Stop!" The toddler was laughing and running even faster when a dark-haired woman rounded the corner of the hallway and nearly tripped over him.

"Oh my! I'm so sorry . . . " The woman's voice trailed off as she stared at Miles. Her eyebrows scrunched into one line, and she almost lost her balance.

Rachel recognized the woman from her pictures.

Come on, Ace, hurry up! I don't know what to say!

Some people nearby were staring, while others were oblivious.

Arianna looked at Rachel as if she had never seen a child in the shelter before. "Is . . . is this your son?"

Rachel nodded. "Yes. Come here, Miles."

Miles backed up from the stranger and let his mother pick him up.

"Oh. He . . . he looks so familiar. He looks exactly like someone I once knew," the woman said. Her eyes filled with tears, and she turned away. "Please, excuse me."

Rachel's breath caught in her throat. She knew. Arianna knew.

"Wait. Mrs. Tate?" Rachel squeaked.

The woman turned back around.

At that moment, Ace emerged from the restroom.

"Daddy!" Miles wiggled free from his mother's grasp and ran to his father.

Arianna's gaze locked on Ace, and it appeared as though she might pass out. "Dear Lord in heaven, I . . . must be dreaming. Wh-what is going on?"

Ace scooped Miles into his arms and smiled awkwardly at his birth mother.

"You're not dreaming. It's nice to meet you. This is my wife, Rachel and my son, Miles, and my name is Ace Feller . . . but I believe you know me as Chase Tate."

CHAPTER TWENTY-TWO

God had performed a miracle. It was incredible. The prayer that Arianna had pleaded with the Lord to answer for nearly twenty years had really, truly come true.

The impossible had happened. She was standing face-to-face with her son. She had fantasized about this day for two decades. But that is all it had ever been—a fantasy. She couldn't fully imagine how it would ever be a reality and therefore hadn't anticipated all of the emotions that were uncontrollable in her system right now.

He was a man now. So tall. There was no trace of the chubby cheeks that he'd had the last time she saw him. He could speak now. His voice was low. His eyes were wise, indicating a life and history that she knew nothing about.

She suddenly felt very small.

"It is you. I knew it the moment I saw your little boy." Arianna covered her eyes with her hands and began sobbing. In her peripheral vision she was aware that her son shift awkwardly.

Get a hold of yourself.

"I'm so embarrassed," she said, sniffling. "I just can't believe this."

At the same time, Ace and Rachel walked forward and hugged her. Miles was smashed in between but didn't seem to mind.

"No need to feel embarrassed!" Rachel patted her back. "This is an amazing situation. It is a gift to meet you."

"How . . . how is it that you're here?" Arianna pulled back and looked at her firstborn, still unable to believe that this moment was real.

"Well, if you don't have plans, I'd like to take you and your family out to dinner tonight, and we can talk more—I hate to bother you at work."

Arianna wiped her eyes and then held her son tightly again. "Yes . . . yes, that would be wonderful. I just hate to part with you. I'm afraid if you walk out that door, I might never see you again."

"I promise I'm not going anywhere. We drove here last night from Colorado and are staying at the Fairfield Inn."

"Colorado." Arianna said as though it explained everything. It had always been a mystery—where her son was living. Was he even in the United States? The truth was, he hadn't been terribly far away.

"How about lunch? I really don't think I can stay at work today. I'm going to contact my husband—your father—and we can meet you somewhere in a couple of hours. My daughter—your sister—is actually here at the shelter on her spring break. She's going to be blown away when I tell her the news that she's going to meet the brother that she's always heard about her entire life."

Ace looked at his wife, and they both nodded. "Lunch it is."

—〰—

Alan was spending spring break at home. His legs were propped up in his La-Z-Boy recliner, and he was watching golf on television when Arianna and CeCe came bounding inside.

"Would you just tell me already?!" CeCe was shouting.

"Woah!" Alan jumped. He kicked down his feet and looked at his wife and daughter as if they were the last people he would have expected to walk inside his house.

Arianna was nearly coming out of her skin. "Okay, now I can tell you!"

She was grinning so wide that she thought she might break her jaw. She grabbed a hold of her husband's arm while jumping up and down, screaming joyfully as though she was a child.

"Alan! Alan! It's happened! It's really happened! What we have prayed for since December twenty-first, nineteen-ninety-four!"

Her husband's expression was that of confusion, hope, and fear. "What do you mean, Ari?"

Tears spilled over as Arianna's body shook, and she had to sit down on the couch to calm her trembling legs.

"Chase. Our son. He's alive. And he's wonderful. He's here!"

Alan's Adam's apple bobbed up and down, and the edges of his eyes became red. "Are you sure?"

"I knew it before he even told me. He has a son that looks exactly like he did the last time we saw him. It's uncanny."

"He came to the shelter?"

"Yes."

"We need to contact the DCI. There are sick people in the world. You don't know if it's someone playing a cruel trick."

"We can do that later this afternoon. But first he wants to take us out to lunch. We're meeting at noon. Talk to him and you'll see he's the real deal."

Alan stared levelly into her eyes. "Just don't get your hopes up until they do a DNA test, okay?"

"No way!" CeCe's voice was much more enthusiastic. "I always wondered what it would have been like to have an older brother. How our days together would have been. Who this kid was. You mean I actually get to meet him?"

"Yes! The wait is finally over! We trusted God, and he has given us the best reward! Chase goes by Ace now, and he is a beautiful man—healthy, polite, a husband, a father . . . oh, if you'll excuse me, I need to go freshen up. It only happens to be the biggest day of my life!"

Alan's face looked pained. Arianna understood his hesitation. He was always careful; she had known him for twenty-four years, and he'd never made a rash or impulsive decision. For the past decade, he'd been the first to admit his flaws and was the most humble Christian that she knew, but he still didn't make choices based on feelings; rather, he took his time weighing all sides of logic. She, on the other hand, didn't find it necessary to always play devil's advocate. She wasn't let down any more if she got her hopes up compared to not at all. In fact, it was the opposite. In her opinion, it was okay to be elated now. Even if it turned out that he wasn't her son (which she knew wasn't going to happen), at least she felt excitement. There had never been any leads. In almost twenty years—no hope. Now, he was here! Would his family decide to stay? To live in Des Moines forever? They had so much catching up to do, so much lost time to make up for. This was the happiest day of her life.

—⟋⟋⟋—

They chose Romano's Macaroni Grill for their meeting spot. Chase—or Ace, Arianna supposed she'd have to get used to calling him—arrived with his wife and son.

Alan gasped when he saw the grown man. Just as Miles was a spitting image of Ace, so was Ace to Alan—just with longer hair and without glasses. Alan immediately lost the suspicious expression that he'd had since Arianna first told him the news.

CeCe looked Ace up and down. Arianna put her arm around her daughter and smiled at the Fellers.

"This is your sister, CeCe," she said and then put her other arm around her husband. "And your father, Alan."

The man whom she'd been married to for twenty-two years bent forward as though the wind had been knocked out of him, and he shook his head while grinning. "It can't be . . . but it is . . . it's you. Can I . . . see your hand?"

Ace held up his left palm, showing off the birthmark that his parents had never forgotten. He smiled. "You mean this one?"

Alan welcomed Ace into his arms, and then Ace hugged CeCe. "Nice to meet you," she said politely.

Tears trickled down Arianna's cheeks. It was a heartwarming sight—one that she never thought she would witness on Earth.

Thank you, Lord, thank you!

After the group was seated and food ordered, they exchanged stories about the past two decades. Arianna noticed that Ace reached for his drink with his left hand. The Tates learned about Lacey, her estrangement to the Fellers, and the day that she changed all of their lives forever. The sharing stopped only when their meals were delivered to their table.

"I have been beside myself with worry, wondering what you were going through all of these years," Arianna said as she watched her son take a bite of his pasta dish. "It seemed too good to be true to imagine that you could actually grow up in a healthy, secure home. I am so grateful . . . so very grateful that you are okay!"

After he swallowed, Ace smiled. "Daniel and Lydia are wonderful parents. I grew up with an ideal childhood."

Arianna returned his smile but also felt an ache inside her heart. Yes, from his end, it was all clean. But as she stared at her son . . . the boy who had consumed her life since she found out she was pregnant with him . . . she realized that he was a stranger to her. She had lost years of his life that she could never get back.

Please, God, don't think that I am complaining. I am happier than I've ever been. But it's bittersweet. He's everything I ever could have wanted in a son . . . but I had nothing to do with it. I missed his birthday parties, his high school graduation, his wedding, the birth of his first child . . .

She had to bite her lip or else the tears would start again. The mixture of emotions put her on such a rollercoaster.

"How long do you plan to stay?" Arianna asked hopefully.

"Through the weekend, if that's okay."

"Absolutely. Please, stay forever." She hoped her words didn't sound as desperate as she felt.

Ace took a drink of water while Arianna pulled out a photo album from a sack that she'd carried in—photographs that Ace said he'd assumed he would never see: his birth at the hospital, his first birthday with a Winnie the Pooh cake, playing in a pile of Iowa's autumn leaves . . .

Alan cleared his throat. "I suppose this would be as good a time as any to call the DCI."

He took his cell phone from his pocket and scrolled through his contacts until he found the name of the special agent. Usually, they associated the phone number with bad news. This time, Alan's voice was jovial when he spoke.

"Hello, sir! It's Alan Tate. I believe the day we've been waiting for has finally arrived. I'm sitting in a restaurant with Chase. My son. The kid's all grown . . . he found us."

—〰—

It would take a couple of weeks for the DNA results to confirm Chase's identity, but even the agents at the DCI seemed to lose their skepticism once they spoke with him, saw the birthmark on his hand—and saw his son.

Ace was very glad that he had come to Des Moines and met the people who gave him life. It was obvious from the pictures and videos (they watched a home movie of the first time he rolled over on the floor, his first steps on camera, and of Arianna playing pat-a-cake with him) that the Tates had made him a happy person, and he began to feel love in his heart for this couple who shared so many of his same physical characteristics.

"I don't believe it," he chuckled when he noticed that Alan had the same stride. Daniel and Lydia had always noted that Ace bounced when he walked—he never realized it was genetic.

They were at the Des Moines zoo (thankful that it was a rare warm day, as it had been a long winter and snow was expected again next week). Miles had so enjoyed the animals on the trip, until it was time for his nap and he became cranky.

"I'm sorry," Rachel apologized to the group, as she tied her brunette hair up into a ponytail. "Do you mind if we sit down for a moment?"

"Of course not," Alan replied.

Rachel picked up Miles from the stroller, but he continued to cry.

"I brought something for you," Arianna offered as she unzipped the bag that she was carrying. She turned to Ace and handed him a stuffed brown bear. "This was yours when you were little, your favorite toy. I slept with it for ten years—I guess it helped me to feel closer to you. But now that you're here, I want you to have it. It's not in the best shape, but maybe Miles would like it."

Ace was touched as he took the bear and studied its fraying ears and the faded words of *I Love You* on its belly. Throughout the weekend, he often felt as though he was meeting a part of *himself* for the first time. He could imagine how the toddler boy from the pictures he'd seen had held on to the bear, and he was sad for the confusion and abandonment his child-self must have felt when he was taken from his parents. Being able to touch his favorite stuffed animal was like touching a part of him for the first time that he never realized was missing—but now he felt complete.

"Thank you so much," he said, offering his son the bear.

Miles was distracted immediately. Rachel placed him back into the stroller with the bear, and within minutes he was fast asleep.

Back at the house, Alan and Arianna also gave Ace a bunch of wrapped presents. Most of the Thomas the Train paper was faded and torn; they explained that they had been his gifts under the tree that first Christmas without him.

"I can't believe I'm finally giving these toys to you. I stopped imagining these sorts of fantasies because it was too painful. Please, give them to Miles as well."

"I really appreciate everything you did and are doing for me," Ace responded to Arianna. "I always dismissed thinking about my first two years of life. I thought I'd spent them living on the streets with a mentally ill woman on drugs; it sure feels a lot better to know that time was spent with you."

They showed him the apartment complex where he had lived and the park where he and Arianna had spent so much time. By the end of the weekend, Ace and his family felt they'd had a nice tour of Des Moines.

"It's going to be hard to come down from all of this." Ace hugged his birth parents goodbye. "I am really glad this worked out the way it did."

Alan's grin took up his entire face. "Me too, son. I never thought I'd see you again. We'll plan a trip out there soon. In the meantime, stay in touch—e-mail, phone, however!"

"Absolutely."

CHAPTER TWENTY-THREE

Lydia didn't usually cry as much as she had the past few months. Whether it was her tough upbringing or just her nature, it was the way she'd always been. But, she cried off and on the entire weekend that Ace was in Iowa.

She'd never been one to feel competitive as a mother. She'd embraced God's Word of giving up her reigns to her children's spouses. But, that was because her role would always be unique. Special. Now that Ace had two mothers, she felt a stir of jealousy. Arianna was his blood. Lydia was the sister of a kidnapper.

As a child, Lydia's dad had been the first to leave. Then, her mom had replaced Lydia with Kevin. Finally, Lacey had chosen drugs and a life on the streets rather than to stay with Lydia. Would Ace meet his mother and realize that he'd been in the wrong family all of these years—and be the next to leave her for something or someone else? She wasn't going to kid herself—their lives were never going to be the same.

And yet, neither were the Tates. She mourned every time she imagined what they must have gone through for twenty years. They must hate her.

Daniel was great through her weekend of weeping. On the last night, he turned on the computer and played the song they'd danced to at their wedding. He knelt down on one knee while she lay on the couch with a box of tissues.

"May I have this dance?"

"What are you doing?" She couldn't help but smile.

He gave his hand a twirl, leaving it in front of her to grab hold. She did.

Daniel had always been funny and witty and comfortable in his skin. He was the smartest man Lydia had ever met and the most authentic. They were still the "sickening cute" couple that their minister had labeled them during their wedding. Everyone, including them, had laughed because it was the truth. Their adoration for each other was apparent wherever they went. Not only did they just *look* like they fit together, but their personalities complemented each other in every setting—they brought out the best in each other. Anyone who doubted that God made two people destined to be together, often changed their minds after getting to know Daniel and Lydia.

The two of them swayed to the music, and all of her cares seemed to drift away. She looked into her husband's eyes and knew that with him, and the Lord, all would be well. She firmly believed that God had their best interests at heart and wouldn't leave them alone with this.

When the song was over, Lydia took a step back. "I want to invite the Tates here this Christmas. In fact, I want them to be here for December twenty-first. It's ironic how that has been the worst day of the year for them and yet the best day of the year for us. I believe that God wants our families to come together. Ace has two sets of parents now; we can both be an equal part of his life."

"I'm on board with that. I think we can learn a lot from them, and maybe we can help heal their hearts. We definitely should meet them," her husband agreed.

As if on cue, their doorbell rang. Daniel walked to the front door and opened it. Ace was standing next to Rachel, and Miles was in her arms with his face buried in her shoulder. Their car's ignition was on in the driveway.

"Oh goodness! You're home! What are you doing, stopping by here?" Lydia ran over to her son and wrapped her arms around him.

"We're not here to stay, just wanted to let you know that everything went amazingly well. They're wonderful people."

"I'm so glad, honey." Lydia pulled back. "I know it's still a long time away, but I was just talking with your father about inviting them to join us this Christmas. We'd love to meet them, and I think it's only right that they get to spend Christmas with you this year."

"That's a wonderful idea. They already mentioned that they want to come see where I grew up. I know this must be a little hard on you, but I want to assure you that Arianna is not going to replace you."

You raised a thoughtful, considerate man, Lydia Feller.

It was all she needed to hear. The insecurities that she had been struggling with off and on for three months were gone. Ace was gaining family, not losing any. She looked forward to the Tates being a part of their future.

—⁓—

"I can't believe he's gone again. A weekend was not enough time. I'm not sure what I imagined . . . I guess I never got this far in my fantasies . . . but I'm feeling really selfish," Arianna was saying to Alan seven hundred and forty miles away from the Fellers. She felt as if her heart was bleeding. "I mean, I know he has a life in Colorado. They have jobs, they have responsibilities . . . they didn't know much about us before coming to see us, so I guess I can't blame them for not committing to much . . . but how can I say goodbye as if he's some long lost relative and not know the next time I can hug him again? I want to see him every day for the next nineteen and a half years!"

Alan adjusted his glasses. "I feel the same way."

"Then let's spend the summer there. In his town."

"The entire summer? CeCe's not going to be happy about that."

"In three years she'll graduate and have the freedom to plan her own summers. I think it will be good for her to get to know her brother."

Alan appeared to ponder his wife's words, and then he clapped his hands and stood up. "All right. Let's do it."

—❦—

Each day until the school year was over, the Tates chatted online with Ace. Arianna couldn't get enough of scrolling through his online photo albums. Being able to see pictures of her son now at any moment really helped to heal her heart. She could go back as far as seven years and see him before he got his driver's license. She could even read the highlights of that time. His high school graduation photos showed him wearing an honor sash, while other photographs were of a missions trip to Haiti when he was fifteen. She was proud of the way he'd turned out.

Arianna praised the Lord constantly. He had not only kept Ace safe, but He'd put him with a top notch family. The Fellers all appeared happy in the pictures—whether it was a fall day spent picking out pumpkins at their patch or a summer that they spent at a lake; his siblings looked like clean-cut, wholesome people. There was nothing to find fault with.

Except that she hadn't been a part of any of it.

Her shoulders tensed. An ache of longing pierced her heart. It felt as if dark smoke billowed out and began to sit in her stomach.

How could she move forward with Ace after missing all of the years in his life that made him who he was now?

Were she and Alan doing the right thing by going out there this summer, or should they just let him be—allow him to keep on living his own life? What if God had taken Ace away because it was better for him?

"Don't be ridiculous," Alan said on the drive to Colorado. He winked at his daughter in the rearview mirror. "CeCe's proof."

The fifteen year old rolled her eyes. Arianna was surprised that CeCe hadn't fought their plan to spend two months in Colorado. She worried about their teenager feeling overshadowed by the sudden appearance of her brother. Arianna had made a conscious effort over the years not to build a shrine to Chase—she wanted her daughter to always know that her parents loved their children equally. But, CeCe had also been used to having her parents' full attention; now they were dropping everything in their lives for someone who was a stranger to her.

"No, I want to go. None of my friends can believe this. It's like the coolest thing that's ever happened to anyone at my school."

It had been a little overwhelming at first—the media had jumped on the story and wanted to follow their every move. But, Arianna knew from past experience that the publicity would die down as soon as the next hot topic came up. Still, it was going to be nice to get away for the summer.

They had asked Ace in the spring for his thoughts regarding their summer plan and were relieved that he had welcomed them enthusiastically. In fact, he offered to find the Tates an affordable place to stay, saying he had a friend who rented out a cabin in the mountains and was willing to give them a discount.

Arianna stood beside the hot tub on the cabin's deck and admired Pikes Peak in the distance. It was a view that nearly took her breath away. Inside the cabin was a cozy kitchen and family room with a fireplace, and a hall led to a bedroom, bathroom, and laundry room. There was also a stairway leading up to a loft where CeCe found a reading chair and another bedroom. They didn't foresee having any complaints with the place.

Arianna called Ace to let him know they had arrived.

"Great. My parents would love for you to join us for dinner."

There it was again. The piercing of her heart. *My parents*. But they weren't his parents! She hadn't given him up for adoption. She was his mother, and Alan was his father. It was an act of Satan that had broken up their family. Those years when she had struggled with anger—pushed people away—and nearly left her marriage could have been different. If he hadn't been kidnapped by *that deranged woman,* they would have been a happy family of four.

"How do you know?" Alan asked once Arianna had hung up the phone and expressed her jealousy.

"What do you mean? Of *course* we would have been happier! I mean, no life is perfect, but it would have been a heck of a lot better than spending all of this time with a hole in my heart."

Alan looked outside at the view toward Pikes Peak. "You could be right. Or maybe not. Maybe the strength that we found after the loss of Chase kept us together. Remember how clueless we were those first ten years? Our marriage could have easily fallen apart and left us miserable. And, maybe we took life for granted—look how active you became at the shelter, how many lives you've helped there and with your Mothers of the Missing group. Would you have gotten involved without our experience with Chase?"

"Sure, you can always find a positive in a negative situation, but I don't think you'll ever convince me that this was the better way."

"I'm not trying to convince you of anything. Just remember that we can't see the entire picture. Only God can."

Arianna sighed. For fifteen years, she had been pleased with how she handled bitter feelings. But it was still her Achilles heel. It was harder than ever right now not to revert back to her default.

Remember how it pulled you away from God last time? Remember how it masked your sin so that you didn't even know you were heading down a destructive path until it was almost too late? Learn from the past. Don't make the same mistake twice. Faith is keeping your trust in the Lord, even when life doesn't make sense. You will be surprised at all of the beauty He has in store for your future with your son.

"I'm white knuckling right now, but I will try. I will really try."

CHAPTER TWENTY-FOUR

The street curved around manicured lawns and full, green trees. Arianna almost expected to see bright blue birds flying by, singing a cheerful tune, for the neighborhood looked like something from a Disney movie.

Well, they certainly were able to afford to give Chase more than we ever could have. Good thing he hadn't been found when he was a kid—why would he have ever wanted to come home when he grew up with this?!

Stop it, Arianna.

Alan pulled into the Fellers' driveway and parked the car.

"Beautiful home," he noted.

"Wow," CeCe breathed from the backseat. She had lived in the same house her entire life—the same home her parents had bought almost nineteen years ago.

Well, let's do this, Arianna thought to herself as she opened the SUV door and stepped onto the pavement with her blue sandals. She was wearing a light pink top and navy capri pants. Alan was nearly matching in a navy blue collared shirt and khaki pants. CeCe was in a white, sleeveless sundress and brown sandals.

"Hello!"

The door opened, and Lydia smiled warmly at the Tates. Even though they had never met, Arianna felt as though she knew them from the Internet. They had "introduced" themselves and joined each other's Facebook pages after Ace's visit. Lydia was possibly the most beautiful woman Arianna had ever seen.

"Nice to finally meet you." Arianna started to shake Lydia's hand, but Lydia embraced her in a hug instead. Daniel did the same.

Ace, Rachel, and Miles joined them in the entry way.

Arianna forced herself not to run in the opposite direction. She felt out of place. Would it ever get easier? What happened to the bond that she once had with her son? She had felt closer to him than any human being she'd ever known. Now she felt she was intruding in a stranger's life. She grieved her son all over again. He didn't even go by his name. The child that she'd been so connected with was gone forever. Even though he was finally standing in front of her, he was not the same person.

As strange as it was, she had grown comfortable with missing him. It wasn't a pleasant comfortable by any means, but it was familiar. It was what she was used to. Now she felt incredible anxiety. Her heartbeat hammered in her ears.

Alan tilted his head, looking at her concerned.

Please, Lord, help me get a hold of myself.

"Won't you come take a seat?" Lydia gestured as she walked into their living room. On the coffee table, in front of their couch and chairs, was a stack of photo albums that Arianna recognized from similar albums she had bought in the 1990s.

"We thought you'd be interested in seeing pictures of Ace as a child."

"Yes." Arianna sat tall and straight on the edge of her seat and clasped her hands in her lap just like her mother always had. Her parents and brother were planning their own trip out to Colorado before the summer's end.

Alan sat down beside her and opened the top album. *Christmas 1994.*

Arianna's breath caught. She covered her mouth. She remembered that first Christmas terribly well. It was just days after she'd last seen her baby. She had been so worried about him . . . had held his bear and stared out the window into that snowstorm . . . praying that God would keep him safe.

He'd been fine. Had spent the day playing with new toys like children were supposed to.

"You bought him a present that year?"

Lydia nodded. "It was a chaotic Christmas with my sister's funeral that week, but we didn't want the kids to miss out, including Ace."

"Thank you," Arianna said quietly.

Alan put his hand on his wife's back and rubbed her shoulders. She caught his gaze and noticed there was a wetness in his eyes. Arianna was more at ease knowing that this was hard for him too, but a bead of sweat trickled down her spine.

"Your sister . . . why . . . why do you think she stole him from me? I mean, I heard she was bipolar . . . and on drugs . . . but there are a lot of bipolar drug addicts in the world, and they don't become kidnappers."

Lydia fiddled with her teal earring and looked down at her feet in matching teal shoes.

"I wish I had an answer. I've been struggling with that same question for the past several months. I never thought she could do something like that. We didn't have the best childhood, but it could have been a lot worse. She lost her baby and, for whatever reason, just snapped that day."

"Well, God condemned her right away to hell," Arianna muttered, referring to Lacey's death that night.

Lydia's cheeks flushed pink. Alan coughed and nudged his wife. Everyone else in the room seemed to shrink away.

"I'm sure that God has held her accountable for her actions, but I am certain, Arianna . . . Alan . . . CeCe . . . Lacey did not and would not have hurt Ace. In fact, much of me thinks she would have come to her senses the next morning and confessed to what she did, had she not died. I think it was a horrible tragedy that she passed away before she could tell us that Ace was not hers. She wouldn't have known how to raise a child . . . I think she was just pretending to be a mother so that she could impress me and wouldn't be alone here for Christmas . . . but would have given him back."

Tears rolled down Arianna's cheeks. Alan grabbed her hand and squeezed.

"Why then couldn't God have kept her alive just one more day?" Arianna clenched her jaw. She couldn't hold it back any longer—the feelings of anger and bitterness pushed through her veins like water breaking through a dam. She hated Lacey. She really did. *She, alone, destroyed my family.* Arianna wanted to run through the door and through the neighborhood, screaming like she had done nineteen and a half years ago. But Lydia stopped her.

"You brought an amazing man into this world. Now he's human, don't get me wrong, and no Jesus—but Mary brought an amazing man into this world too." The older woman stood up and looked out the window into the distance. "She had to give him up in order for him to save souls for centuries upon centuries. Do you know what Ace did almost five years ago?"

Arianna answered the question with a shake of her head and accepted a tissue from Rachel for her tears.

"He saved a lot of lives. Here. In Colorado. At our tree farm. If not for him, countless people would have died in a gas explosion. God must think you a very strong and wonderful woman, for he used you to be the vessel to bring Ace into this world."

The Fellers all contributed to the telling of the story, and all Arianna could hear inside her head was that song. "Breath of Heaven" might as well have been her soundtrack for two decades, and it made perfect sense now. She resonated with the lyrics of being frightened by the load she bore . . . in a world as cold as stone . . . feeling as though she walked alone. Only the Breath of Heaven had helped her to be strong. Yes . . . God had known all along. He had been speaking to her through that song for almost twenty years.

She blinked. "Wow."

"Wow," Alan repeated.

Arianna had tried to convince herself that anything good to come out of her son's kidnapping was simply "looking on the bright side," which felt . . . lame, to put it bluntly. This news was different. She had been looking at the tragedy through her own filter, but what about what was best for the lives of so many others? Or the purpose that God had for Ace? Even to marry Rachel and have Miles. Did Arianna really think that *she* knew best?

Her shoulders relaxed. Miles, who had been swinging around the *I Love You Bear*, pulled the string, and "Twinkle, Twinkle Little Star" began its tune.

"I've never seen that little guy before," Lydia said. She reached out and touched the top of the bear's head.

"It was Ch-*Ace's* when he lived with us," Arianna said.

Lydia raised her eyebrows. "Really? Because that's the only song that comforted him during his first year here. He would cry out for you . . . I thought he missed Lacey . . . but it was you. He stopped crying when I played that song."

Happy tears caught in Arianna's eyes. Lydia's words were a gift. The imaginary smoke inside of her heart evaporated. She hadn't gone back to being a slave to anger and bitterness after all. In fact, she'd never been this peaceful.

CHAPTER TWENTY-FIVE

Aside from visiting Pikes Peak, the Garden of the Gods, Cave of the Winds, and numerous other tourist attractions in Colorado Springs during their summer, Alan and Arianna got to know Ace and formed a new, close bond with him.

They often had dinner at his house with Rachel and Miles, while other times Alan joined Daniel for fishing, and Lydia took Arianna around to nearby stores for shopping.

It was an unlikely match, but the families were appreciative of the friendship that had formed between them.

On the Fourth of July, the Tates were able to meet Jason, Monica, Miranda, and Tori, who all stayed for a week before heading back to their various homes. They sat on a blanket at a local park and shared buckets of fried chicken, mashed potatoes, baked beans, coleslaw, macaroni salad, a veggie tray, and chips. For dessert, Lydia made a sheet cake that was decorated like a flag, while Arianna made red, white, and blue layered rice cereal treats, which the children enjoyed.

Jason was twenty-eight and had been married for two years. He and his wife lived in Illinois with their fourteen-month-old daughter.

Monica and Miranda were twenty-five and still lived on opposite coasts. Monica had gotten married three years ago and had a daughter just a couple of months older than her niece. Miranda was happy being single.

Tori, who was ready to start her junior year of college in Colorado Springs, wasn't entertaining thoughts of marriage either.

As Arianna looked around at Miles playing with his cousins, she felt her heart grow warm. This was where Chase—Ace—was meant to be. The Fellers' business was successful, and one day he would be the sole owner.

"What do you think about moving here after CeCe graduates from high school?" Arianna asked her husband when they returned to their cabin after the fireworks. She held her breath, bracing herself, expecting him to say that it was impossible. After all, he'd taught at the same school for twenty years. It was a good district, and he had a longstanding reputation in the community as both a teacher and girl's track coach. The Tates had been born and raised in Iowa and had planned to stay there for the rest of their lives.

"I have been thinking the same thing."

Arianna breathed out through her nose. "You have?"

Alan stuck his hands in his pockets. "Yeah. Being here feels right. Being with my son again feels right. We don't have any more time to lose. We missed out on nearly twenty years of his life. If it's God first, family second, and everything else after that, then it'll all work out. If Ace gives us his blessing, of course."

Not only was Ace thrilled by the news, but so were Daniel and Lydia. They offered to help in whatever way they could. Even CeCe remarked about Colorado's beauty and said that she was interested in applying to colleges there. Alan hoped that preparing two years for their move would allow him to find a decent teaching job. It would also give Arianna time to say goodbye to the friendships she'd made at the shelter and Mothers of the Missing group. Her parents and brother gave her reason to still visit Iowa, but she had come full circle when it came to living in Des Moines.

Knowing that their home would be near their son very soon made saying goodbye at the end of the summer a whole lot easier.

"The invite still stands—I hope you will join us for Christmas," Lydia said as the families hugged goodbye.

"Absolutely. Thank you so much for making us feel at home here. We look forward to returning in a few months."

The two women, both of whom had worried about competition with each other, had recognized that they were allies. Their smiles for each other were genuine. Arianna was grateful to Lydia for listening to the Holy Spirit, or they might not be here now. Her insistence at searching for answers year after year led her to finding the truth.

Arianna squatted down and slid her arms around Miles. It was a gift that he looked so much like Chase. She hadn't been able to watch her son grow up, but she would be there to see her grandson.

Ace embraced her as she stood back up, and Arianna used her hand to brush her son's curls away from his blue eyes, just as she had done when he was a toddler. "Every Christmas I wondered if it was going to be the last one that I spent without you. Now I know . . . the twentieth Christmas was the last. What a blessing the year 2014 has been."

"Thank you for never giving up on me." Ace looked at both Alan and Arianna. "I love you, Mom. I love you, Dad."

It was the first time he'd ever referred to them by those titles, and the first time they'd ever heard him speak the phrase. It was music to Arianna's ears, and she knew it was just the beginning.

Thank you, Lord. Thank you for not giving up on me.

"We love you, too, son."

THE END